THE SHOE COBBLER
WHO MENDED SOULS

"Michael Paul Collett has told a remarkable story
that will inspire readers with his illuminating message
about the infinite possibilities life unfolds."

Marci Shimoff
Co-author, *Chicken Soup for the Woman's Soul*
Featured teacher in hit film, *The Secret*

THE SHOE COBBLER
WHO MENDED SOULS

Michael Paul Collett

Hughes Henshaw Publications
Palm Bay, FL 32907 USA

Hughes Henshaw Publications

THE SHOE COBBLER WHO MENDED SOULS

First Hughes Henshaw Publications edition published 2007.
Font Centaur MT 12 point by Linotype, Germany.
Cover Art Vincent Van Gogh, Dutch, 1853-1890
A Pair of Boots, 1887, Oil on canvas, 13 x 16 1/8 in. (33 x 41 cm.)
The Baltimore Museum of Art: The Cone Collection, formed by Dr. Claribel Cone and Miss Etta Cone of Baltimore, Maryland BMA 1950.302

ISBN I-892693-18-6   ISBN 978-I-892693-18-I

Library of Congress Control Number: 2007926579

Collett, Michael Paul
   The Shoe Cobbler Who Mended Souls / Michael Paul Collett
     p. cm
   Summary: "A shoe cobbler discovers his own soul through losses, failures, disappointments and opportunities. He learns what the true meaning of miracles are, and becomes the person he strives to be by understanding the difference between knowledge and wisdom. He grows in the understanding of the true meaning of life through his myriad experiences." – Provided by the publisher.
ISBN I-89-26-93-18-6 (5.5 x 6.75) alk. paper)
I. Visionary   2. Spiritual life 3. Self-actualization

Hughes Henshaw Publications
424 Hurst Road NE • Palm Bay, FL 32907 • 321.956.8885
e-mail: hugheshenshaw@aol.com • www.hugheshenshaw.com

DEDICATION

I dedicate this book to Daphna Moore.
Without her inspiration and annoying persistence
and loving encouragement this book would not exist.
Thank you my friend.

 PART ONE

It was still dark, early morning, when he gathered his gear and moved as quietly as possible through her cottage. The journey he was about to make demanded all of his focus.

He left a letter for her on the kitchen table. She would see it as soon as she began her morning routine. At first, it would not surprise her, for he often awakened early and went out into the morning to pray and clear his mind. He would say he was awakening with nature from the darkness within, to once again be of service in God's light of day. But often times he would question which were really the darkest hours; those of the night, or those of man's deeds during the day. His mind went over the letter as he walked.

I do not know why I do what I do, but it is such a pull or almost a push one could say. It is as if my soul cries out for the punishment of my solitude, or absence from you. It is not something I can fight and win, all of the time. It is as if something from some unknown place pushes me out your door when I lie there at night mentally clinging to what I want. Sometimes I awaken and feel my hands gripping the hewed wood of the bed frame, as if I am fighting to hang on until the light, so I will not have to face the darkness.

Please know that I love you, more than I have said, for it almost steals the beat from my heart when I try to speak of it. The mornings when we awaken together and you take a blanket to wrap your nakedness and stand in the window and let the early morning light dance off of your hair and skin, I marvel at the beauty that God has allowed to stand before me, the beauty of body and soul that chooses to share time with me. I love just sitting in the same room with you and watching you read by the fire. The smell of fresh flowers that seem to come from your hair when I kiss your neck, I have yet to tell you, but to just lay my face on your left shoulder and have my lips against your neck is a place I could stay for a very long time. Oh yes, I was not kidding when I spoke of that spot just above your knee on your inner thigh, how silky smooth it is. Just amazing places I have come to find with the touch, lying there, breathing you in when we fall asleep, both tired from reading and talking of the day's events.

My love, my feelings for you are, or must be, a sin, for I am surely weakened and distracted by your being. But then it may also be a blessing that keeps me grounded in a common or seemingly safe reality. Just know that I love you, and when I understand this action that calls me away, then maybe I can leave it behind or share it more openly in word with you.

Just so you know, today I go for the rock wall that lay in the north shadows, the one I have pointed at in the past. I will return in two days.

Love you.

P. S. A surprise awaits you; it is hidden behind your books on the shelf above the wood stacked on the hearth. I had it made for you in the village.

"Excuse me, excuse me."

He turned, looked, and there stood a customer at the counter. Everything was gone, she was gone, and all that remained was the present. He put down the boot he was working on, laid down his hammer, and waited on the customers standing in line who needed leather or shoes repaired.

He realized the visions or dream states had moved to a different stage or level. It was almost out of his control; as if anything ever was in your control he thought. When he finished helping the last customer, he picked up the next boot and began to set the nails in the shank area of the boot sole. He laughed to himself, it seemed it was always one type of soul work or the other—his own soul, or the soles of boots and shoes that carried each individual on their journeys throughout their lives.

By the time the fourth nail was placed in the heel, as he nailed the rubber heel cap to the base of the boot, it happened again. That ringing sound of the metal shoe last, holding the boot in place as it was nailed, found a new rhythm in his mind—the sound of a metal pin, a piton being driven into the crack of the rock.

note. He realized she had to have gotten up very early and packed this, she had to have been awake the entire time.

His gaze immediately turned and tried to focus on the farm setting, but all he could see was the familiar meadow where it was nestled.

Hesitantly he unfolded the note; the writing was definitely in her hand. It was neatly written, without pretense, but he felt the words deep into his very core.

> *By now, you must be halfway to the top. I pray all is well. I want you to know that I love the way you make me feel when we are together. I have never been treated as you treat me, so caring and you are usually focused on me or us. But, I want you to know that when I start seeing that certain look, no, not that look where you think you can pull me into bed anytime you want. I understand that look; it is the other look you have at times, so abandoned, or distant, as if you are searching for where you belong, where you can live free. Please talk to me, I am a good listener, I hear more than you think, even when you say nothing. So climb on, I'll see you tomorrow. Climb well and focus on safety and success. I am in love with you. Yes, it is true.*
>
> *There is much to share. I have things I need to show you, we can be more in time.*
>
> *Love you.*

"Hey! Could I get some help here?!"

His hand dropped the hammer to the floor; his counter was once again alive with impatient customers. A woman stepped to the counter and explained what she needed. He filled out the ticket then placed the shoes on the "work to do" shelf. Another woman stepped forward and was upset because the process was taking so long. She began by demanding that certain things be done to her very expensive fashion shoes and boots, and if they were not completed as she requested, there would be a problem. He brushed his hands off on his apron, looked over her boots and shoes, then looked up at her with a grin, more of a smile in his eyes, and said, "No, it could not be done as requested." Of course the woman was taken aback.

She said, "It is obvious you have never heard the phrase, the customer is always right."

He calmly looked at her, like a predator, a cat playing with a mouse, his anxiousness to attack barely held in check.

With amazing calm, he asked the woman, "Have you ever worked on shoes or attempted any shoe repair training?"

She snapped back, "Of course not."

Then he smiled at her and said, "Then you know nothing of your demands, and in this case, the customer is not right. So anytime you come in here as long as I am here, you will never be right. Furthermore, to do what you ask, even if I would consider it, you could not afford me. Your request is ridiculous to say the least, and it would be a waste of my time."

By then, her body temperature had risen at least ten degrees and she was gasping out of frustration for intelligent words, which he knew would never come. She finally blurted out, "NO ONE has ever spoken to me this way before! Do you know who I am?"

At that point his whole manner changed, she sensed a strange change, a difference, but knew not what to do. He spoke calmly and clearly so the rest of the customers could hear, for they did know her and seemed aware of her self-importance. "I don't care who you think you are and it is certainly amazing to me that no one has ever talked to you in this manner before, because if you come back tomorrow I'll do it again so you can begin to understand your proper place in the scheme of things."

That was the final blow. She grabbed her boots and shoes and stomped out of the shop.

Looking up, he said, "Next."

An older gentleman laid down some money and a ticket. He requested to pick-up his boots. After looking over the work, he complimented the shoe cobbler on his skill and smiled. He said, "You are not only skilled in your craft but you are also entertaining. Have you ever considered politics?"

The cobbler replied, "I would never do anything to diminish the integrity of this trade." Then they both laughed and the gentleman went on his way vowing to return with more work.

"Maybe I'll bring a lunch next time," he replied when he got to the door, "I could use some new philosophical insight and more live entertainment."

The cobbler waved goodbye, grabbed a bite of food and some tea and went back to work. He could not understand what was happening to him. Everything seemed to be changing; energies, thoughts, and patterns of work. A change was coming; he could feel it. He finished the last pair of boots and took a break. He needed some time off, just go away for a while he thought, as he took another bite of food.

His feet were roughly 1,000 feet above the ground; he was staring at the valley, holding a note in his hand. Realizing he was back on the ledge, he was back, back from what? To what? The note was folded and placed back in the pack, as was the food. He knew now what must be done. He secured his gear and began visually checking the rock face for a way to continue. He could not go down, he had to finish. She would want him to finish.

He began the climb once again, but now with more effort. He made up his mind to be back by morning, not two more days. He climbed in a controlled but aggressive style, totally focused, moving smoother and gaining ground by the minute. One hundred feet lay to the summit, still he had roughly four hours of daylight left, he could make it, and he would make it. His position became precarious, his exposure was extreme, roughly 1,700 feet up, on a very smooth section about twenty feet long, and he was stuck. Panic approached, but he fended it off by controlling his breathing. Then he saw it, a small hole and a tiny crack about three feet from his reach.

Suddenly his mind began asking questions; then another part of him began answering them. It was as if he was only a vehicle for two passengers.

"Why are you really here? What purpose does this serve?"

"I'm at peace, not harming anyone," came the answer. "I enjoy this!"

"But you are afraid," was the reply. *"What purpose does it serve?"*

"Life. I am living, seeing, feeling, and learning things about myself that I would not know. The more I know, the better I can understand myself; and communicate to others."

"You really mean you are just feeding the ego, don't you!?"

Then it hit him and he began to doubt. What if something happened? Would she still love him? Why would he intentionally put himself in these positions of risk when he only wanted to be with her, to share life, and to love her?

Now he froze, the fear got him. His thoughts were like a grass fire in the mid-summer's heat. His throat had closed and had a foul taste in it. The worst kind of fear, panic so chaotic that a pattern had to reveal itself before any resolution could be found.

He heard the inner voice, "Reach for it, completely relax your body and reach."

His fingers found purchase in the tiny crack, his foot found a small nub that seemed to appear out of nowhere. He slowly pulled himself upward, placed protection, and began to move again, upward until he pulled himself over the final edge. He gathered himself together and just sat and looked on the world that lived below. They say no man is an island, but to him it seemed that all things below were operating quite well without him.

Then it came to him. It was not the world and people below he could not adjust to, it was himself. He did this because of his need to find himself, to find an image, a hope, an identity. All of this was to prove to himself that he was, was what? What did he really want?

To be at peace, if love was there, or not, so be it.

To put everything on someone or something else never worked. Something else was never enough; more and more, higher and harder climbs, different friends or women. What was it? What is happening to me?

He gathered his gear and began the long hike down the opposite side. Maybe one day in the future he would understand the needs of the starving soul; or was it the ego? He felt he wanted to be with her, more than before. His pace quickened as the descent leveled off and he found the main road. It was just getting dark, but he did not care, the five miles remaining he knew well on this road. He settled into a good rhythm.

A couple of hours passed and then he saw the light of her cottage. There was a small fire glowing in front of the house. He started walking faster hoping everything was okay. As he came near the gate she stood up and said, "I thought we could cook out tonight, you know, kind of like a late picnic."

Then she smiled a smile that made her face light up, and kissed him on the cheek.

How did she know, he thought. I was not coming back for a couple of days. He started to say something but she kissed him softly on the lips and said, "I know a lot," as if she had read his mind. "Please sit, throw down your gear, and let's eat by the fire. We have much to talk about, but for now it can wait."

She had everything prepared, everything, and as he turned he saw in the shadow of the flames she had even moved the wooden bed outside under the stars of the cool and clear night. His entire being was elated, still confused, but in love with it all.

After they had eaten, they soaked in a nearby hot springs, came back, and climbed under a pile of blankets on the large wooden frame bed.

It was then as they were lying together, looking up at the stars, when she began to talk.

"Look," she said. "I love you, but I am not in love with you because of what you do, it is because of who you are, and that my dear is something you do not know. That is your problem, which is why you do what you do. I don't like you up there alone, risking yourself for some personal insight, but I can't tell you not to go. We are together to share our lives, like you said, not change each other to another's ideals. Would you take me up there next time?"

"No," he replied.

"Why not?" she asked.

"I would never risk anything happening to you, and if I made a mistake and harm came to you I don't know if I could handle it."

"You told me there are women climbers a lot better at climbing than you; you've even climbed with women. Why not me? Am I some kind of possession that only gets used in a safe environment?"

"No," he said as he turned to face her. "You just mean so much to me, and I went through so much before God granted me this gift. How could I foolishly risk it?"

She smiled the smile that means: Can you hear your own words?

"Then why are you putting yourself at foolish risk?" she asked him.

It hit him, crushing his chest so that the breath escaped but did not return without conscious effort. She was right, without her, he would not have this shared happiness; but without himself, or whole self, he also would not have this same shared happiness.

"So," he said, "do you want to teach me how to farm?"

"Maybe we could try climbing easier, less risky mountains or cliffs," she answered. "Maybe both. But know that I am not one of those women who have to be with someone, a man, to provide me with security. I love life, as you do, but I connect with it in a different way. Share with me my way for a while and let us see how you feel. But remember I love you for who you are, not what you do. I will help you find out what that is, as you help me, as you have in the past. See, all this time you had no idea how much you were doing for me. What do you say partner? Want to give it a try?"

Then with a laugh, she pulled the blankets over their heads. In the dark and warmth of the blankets under the clear night sky, she pushed his face slowly into that spot on her neck and he felt that silky smooth place of her inner thigh slowly move up and around his waist.

He could smell fresh coffee, he could hear her saying,

"Get up farm boy, there is work to do."

She was standing there handing him a cup of hot coffee, and the only thing she was wearing was one of his long-tailed flannel shirts, her loosened hair glistening from the early morning sunlight.

When he opened his eyes, he was sitting up in his own bed, outstretched arm and hand reaching for something and for someone who was not there. But the smell of coffee was!

Once he realized he was actually in his own bed, alone, thousands of miles away, or was it lifetimes away, he was crushed; his thoughts were shattered, had she really existed, had any of it? But the smell of coffee? For two days he would not talk. What happened?

The usual customers did not know how to communicate with him any longer, nor did the people that saw him daily. Something had happened to him.

The shoes came and went, his smile slowly returned, but now something was missing in him.

Days turned into weeks. He returned to the studies of the past, studies he no longer wished to participate in: astrology, shamanism, seers, various works of the mind pertaining to communication, even dreams. He had hoped to drop it all and find a somewhat peaceful path to God. Was this one more obstacle to overcome? Could this be part of his journey through God's design? He did not know. How could he? The finite could not contain in boundary the infinite, anymore than you could put the ocean in a single teacup.

His mannerisms changed, he let his hair grow longer and longer, he grew a mustache. His diet changed and he began losing weight. People began to worry about him. He worked, prayed, and seemed to always be in deep thought. The doors were being closed. He shunned organized religion, social gatherings, and eventually society, a piece at a time. He focused on his work, which became better and better. People who used to come and seek him out for viewpoints were shunned or repulsed. He would tell them to meditate until they heard a popping sound. The popping sound would represent their heads being pulled out of their behinds, and after moments of adjusting to the light, they should be able to begin their journey, awake with vision and clarity. Just go experience your own life and leave me alone.

Of course he offended them, and they began to leave him alone, other than for his trade. He was withdrawing from what he referred to as their intentional ignorance.

He thought if it didn't come quick and with an order of French fries most people did not want it, no matter what they looked for. They seemed so caught up in the ego's desire of material gain, or to be recognized as special in this world, that they would miss the subtle energies working in harmony all around them. So life slowly shifted to the mundane, the seemingly ordinary existence that people feel they are in, but really are not. He was aware, and waiting like a predator who knows something, knows that some prey has entered its immediate environment. The muscles would stretch and flex as he worked, went for walks, even at meals. His eyes were squinting as if he was always looking into something that was far away or not there at all. He even smelled the air, testing for a fragrance or taste that would reveal what was taking place. His senses finally gave out after weeks of vigilance, his entire being had been exhausted and he collapsed.

One day after work he went home, took off his shoes, washed his face, and sat down to catch his breath before making something to eat. His body gave in and he slept, never waking for twenty-three hours, then, when he stirred, he was disoriented. His body was stiff and sore, and he was very hungry.

He got out of bed, his body would not respond to the request the mind was asking of it. He shaved and showered, tried to do some light stretching and a workout but all was to no avail. He made himself some snacks from fresh fruit, potatoes, avocados, and chicken. He took the food and a book, walked to his truck, and intended to drive out into the desert for a while, but ended up at the shoe repair shop. It did not seem to matter that it was his day off. He parked the truck, unlocked the door to the shop, and locked it behind him after he had stepped into the dark. He stood in the dark and just felt the building, the energies. He breathed in the smell of the tanned leathers and glue; the smells of waxes and ink were more subtle.

He laughed to himself. This was his home, his haven of comfort and peace.

Setting down the food on the workbench, he turned on all the lights, turned on some music, sat down, and ate his meal. Now he could play the music loud to get the full melody of the strings of the violin. He loved classical music, all kinds, traditional from different cultures, to the various instruments they used.

Today he played one of his favorites, Max Bruch's Violin Concerto No. 1 in G Minor, Op. 26. The music motivated him as he sat and ate and just listened and felt the notes of the melody and intermitting silences move through him. The shoe shop had always been very clean and organized, especially for a shoe repair shop. Everyone commented on it, especially those who had owned, worked in, or just had dealings with shoe repair. But as the music changed and he finished his food, he stood up and began to clean even more.

After hauling out two trash buckets full of shoe boxes from the boot section, he began taking apart the machines, one by one, cleaning and oiling. Then he got to the one machine he named Ole Big, it was a Landis 12-L shoe and boot stitcher. It was used to sew the soles onto boots and shoes that were welted, called Goodyear Welting, Norwegian Welting or "turned out" welting, which is a European style welting that is stitched to the edge of the sole. The cowboy boot is one such boot. You see the stitching on the edge or top of the sole. It was a strip of leather fastened, by sewing, externally to the forefoot or in some cases all the way around the boot or shoe. After the shoe was repaired and the new sole glued on, the sole was sewn by placing the boot or shoe on the machine, and by guiding it around the shoe as the Landis-L sewed a heavy thread through the sole and welt.

This machine was powerful and its mechanics always left him in awe of the inventor. He always liked to keep on good terms with all of the tools and machines in the shop. From the time of his childhood he had known, he had either been involved in this craft or would be in the future, or both. Anyway, he had always heard that shoe shops had a special magical quality that existed in them. He believed it, because it had been shown to him more than once in his experiences.

One day a machine had broken down. He could see the problem, but after working on it for several hours he sat down, hungry and tired, and looked at the clock. It was one o'clock in the morning; he had been working seventeen hours straight.

Finally, he gave in to his exhaustion and said out loud, "God, I know you are busy and this is not something that you generally deal with, but I sure could use some help here. I can't do it alone. Maybe if you have a helper not busy, I would sure appreciate it. Amen."

As he sat there, in the peripheral vision he saw something, almost like a shadow, but transparent. He felt its presence. He felt something had taken place, so he decided to try the machine once more, even though he had put it all back together he had not gotten it to function. It began operating better than before, and he knew this was the magic old cobblers and writers through time had spoken of. He thanked God and His helper for the blessing. He was then so inspired he found some paint from a previous job, repainted the walls, finished cleaning, and sharpened his hand tools.

He realized now, this work with its material and spiritual connection was his true grounding in life because it served a good purpose. It helped humankind as a whole and instilled humbleness and focus in him as if he were doing his work for or unto God, as the scriptures say. There were many moments of clarity and magic for him in the shop from then on. This was one place he did not have to wear a mask. This was his opus, slowly being revealed through the present medium.

The cobbler had run out of tickets to keep track of items left for repair. As he retrieved a new bundle from beneath the counter, a woman approached and asked his name. Always suspicious of people's nature, he in turn asked her why she needed to know. She told him her name and why she was there. She said that some people he had befriended, a couple of her associates, had suggested she talk with him about a problem she was having, if he had time. His response was that he fixed shoes and was not a shrink.

Smiling and stepping forward she said, "That is how my associates described you, evasive and blunt."

She had been pre-warned not to be offended.

Watching her body language for a moment, seeing her eyes take things in, and how her breathing was all in the upper part of her body and almost being held in at times, she seemed proud, strong, confident in her manner and physical appearance.

Finally speaking he said, "Well, it is quiet now, maybe I'll take a short break and chat with you if you would choose to."

She agreed and they stepped away from the counter. She said her companion, the man she was romantically involved with, had recently left her for no reason. She was having a hard time dealing with the anguish of his departure. Her aloneness was overwhelming. It was beginning to affect different aspects of her daily life, even her work; and since she was directly involved with people the result of this action was beginning to show negative results with her clients.

He listened until she stopped speaking; her hands never stopped squeezing the purse that she carried.

Then she looked directly at him, "Can you share any kind of guidance with me?"

Her speech was restrained, but she spoke professionally; he began to admire her need to understand.

"You had better set your purse down, or at least sit down before I do try speaking to you," he said.

"I prefer to stand for I cannot stay long and I do not want to interrupt your day too much," she replied.

"You will drop your purse when I answer you. Just relax, lower your breathing, and take deeper breaths."

She shifted her weight on her feet, at that moment he spoke.

"There is a reason that your so-called companion left. You know what it is, you just don't want to accept it. Your pride won't allow it. Can you blame him anyway?"

Her eyes narrowed, her lips pressed together as she inhaled sharply. She began to respond vocally, and as she did, her purse fell from her hands. Startled, she just stood and stared at him.

"How did you know?" she asked.

"How can you expect to know anyone else if you don't know yourself?"

Without giving her time to answer, he continued.

"You cannot even control your own actions when it becomes overly challenging to your emotions. So how is it you believed you could control a relationship or someone else in the relationship? As soon as I made you slightly angry, which I did intend to do, you forgot the physical strain you were placing on a part of yourself, and therefore, dropping the purse was the result. You mentally needed to redirect that energy to another facet of yourself for defense and to retaliate, proving that being out of control is a threat to you. In life there is very little you can actually control.

The only thing in control of anything is God. You can be in control of your choices of free will, but other than that, you are giving yourself far more power than you actually are capable of. The word you may be seeking is flow. The flow of your life always has a direction. Sometimes in your choices used in free will, you come into conflict or chaos with this flow. These are nothing more than stimuli or road signs letting you know you have drifted out of the flow, sort of like those small bumps on the edge of a highway that make a growling noise when your tires go out of the lane too far to one side. Forget your companion, this is about you. Now I have a question for you if I may, and since you are still standing here I'll take that as a yes."

She began to form tears in her eyes as she bent to pick up the purse.

"Stop! Leave it for now, you don't need a pacifier, you need you. The question is, if you could have either your companion back or your heart and self back, which would you choose?"

After a moment of thought she answered.

"I guess I would choose him because he took my heart."

Quickly bending down and picking up her purse, wiping it off, and handing it to her, he smiled and said, "I am sorry, but there are no words I know that can help you."

As he turned away from her, he said, "It was nice to have met you," and he started working again.

The woman started to cry and said, "You did not even tell me your name."

"It is not important," he replied, as he put the repair tickets on a spindle and closed the cabinet door. "I hope your day improves," and he bid her good day.

"Wait," she said, as tears were falling down her cheeks like a small child who was punished for something she did not do. She had that look of anxiety and bewilderment mixed with innocence.

He turned on her immediately. "What man could be worth your heart as a souvenir or token? No one can take something of this nature unless it is given, and that is what you have done; intentionally I know not, but given nonetheless. Don't you see? In all your daily activities you have described as being out of harmony, the thing missing of most importance is not him, but you my friend, the whole of you. The heart that is missing was not taken, it was misplaced by you when you attempted to control the relationship. He did not take it. You gave it away in the selfish act of control. A relationship is meant to be shared, two together sharing in harmony, whole lives individually sharing, not wanting to intentionally change, control, or harm another. Your loss of heart was your price to pay for your selfish act. You can, however, correct it quite easily. You must forgive him for the reason that you began to doubt in him, and you must forgive yourself for trying to keep and control what is not yours to hold on to. We all are meant to be free in God's eyes. It is our own poor choices that make us prisoners. Now answer the question with truth and clarity. Which would you choose to have back, you or your absent companion?"

This time without hesitation she meekly replied, "I would choose to have myself back."

They spent an hour talking; she went into his work area and sat down. As he continued working, customers came and went, never suspecting anything. She acknowledged a couple dropping off a pair of boots to be repaired.

As they left, she looked at him. "You sure touch many souls during the day don't you?"

He laughed heartily and held up a pair of boots with holes worn through the bottom.

"They even come in pairs," he said jokingly.

"That's not what I meant," she replied.

"I know, and it was very kind of you to say something like that. However, the answer is no, I try not to. In the beginning, I felt it was the thing to do, then my ego became involved in the process a little too much, getting me into trouble, or I should say, unnecessary problems. Then I was shown to not offer anything at all, unless approached as you have done, just to be as kind as possible, get their work, and get them out of my space. I am beginning to see that is the best way. Most people are so unaware of themselves, let alone their surroundings that one usually wastes sixty-five percent of the conversation on an unfocused mind."

"Is that why you are so blunt at times, or is it that you just don't like people? I hear you spend most of your time alone when you are not here working."

He was surprised at her information; he studied her carefully before he answered. Then he said, "I am without human companionship, but I am never alone, is what should be said. I have my own answers to work on, my own chaos to find my way through. Personally, I have been told I am too intense and can become too distant to be around. I don't blame them; sometimes I even envy them in a way. No matter how hard I try I cannot be like them. I think most of us would like to go, once again, to that place where we felt elusive happiness with someone in our lives, when we actually thought we knew who we were, and what a wonderful place we were in, in our relationship."

"You don't feel like that anymore?" she asked.

"I am not sure I ever did. Nevertheless, I have wondered about it, listening to other people's stories or reading some of their books. I haven't decided if they are just very naive or I am just cynical."

Then they both laughed. She said she should go and thanked him. "You gave me a lot to think on and I will work on it."

He thanked her for her company, walked her to the door and locked it behind her. There was still work to do, and it was his favorite time in the shop, when all of the distractions were gone.

Walking back to the workbench he pulled out an apple and his favorite potato chips, food of the mind; disturbed mind, he thought to himself. He started laughing and cutting worn-out soles from boots and shoes. He cleaned the inner shoes, sanded them down, picked out the old stitches on the welts, checked the shanks, did all the small tedious tasks that take place in the process of soleful revival during the journey of the boots and shoes, and put in the new linings.

The gluing process completed and the new soles attached onto the footwear, they were shaped and made ready for one of the final steps in securing the new sole to the body of the shoe or boot. For the sewing process that takes place, he moved over to Ole Big, the Landis 12-L stitcher. He checked the wax pot for thread wax; checked the bobbin thread, needle, and awl; and set the correct stitch length for the type of work to be done to how many stitches per inch would be used to help secure the sole in place.

Turning on the machine, he began sewing. After sewing a couple of pairs of boots he felt light headed from not eating enough that day, so he finished and sat down. The sound and rhythm of the stitcher still echoing in his mind, he began to feel even stranger, his hands began to feel odd, then peculiar odors filled his senses; smells and feelings that were not of his usual day in the shop.

He began to shake as if a damp cold had permeated deep into his body. The air smelled strange, clammy, and even moldy. Surrounded by the tainted smell of urine and gunpowder, his eyes began to focus on terrible scenes, as if in a movie or the memory of a movie. Realizing it was not any movie he was recalling, but an actual experience, time and clarity revealed his location, some sort of trench, wet and muddy. He could not tell if it was spring or fall, somewhere once again in the distant past.

He found himself hidden among debris, shattered tree branches, mud everywhere, and all types of spent casings from weapon fire. Then he began seeing the bodies laying around him, as if in a play on a stage, all waiting for the curtain to drop so the grisly scene can be cleaned up and the play could continue with the next act. Here there were no actors though; none were getting up and changing for the next scene. The smell was increasing as the sun rose higher and higher among the clouds in the gray sky. He was at war; why and where? His mind raced. Then he heard a language not readily understood by him, but not unfamiliar either.

He realized by his place in the rubble and his state of being he was hiding from whoever was coming. Somehow, this person, this being understood it all, knowing it was just a small surge of adrenaline preparing him for the task ahead. He let go of any attachments, for the simple reason that he feared he would not live if he did not, so he became the vision.

As he became absorbed into the new reality, he began to experience a new awareness. His sense of hearing and smell increased greatly. The state of his mind went from fear to calculation. As moments passed, he realized he was not the prey after all, he was the predator.

Waiting, somehow he knew the tables of life had turned, for the original predator that had been subdued in its aggressiveness had now become the prey.

Slowly, ever so slowly, he pressed himself deeper into the walls of the muddy trench, mingling without thought with the soulless bodies already scattered. His hands were relaxed, yet the right hand held an object. He slowly lowered his eyes to confirm its identity. A knife, a small odd-looking knife, was in his right hand; his left hand was folded into a relaxed fist. He noticed how the palm was completely clean and dry, as if it were intentionally kept that way for a purpose.

The language had gotten louder, and then in the mist, he could see shapes, slowly taking form, becoming clearer as they continued to approach. He could feel his muscles coiling, ready to strike. It was then that he became certain of his present duties. Two men emerged from around the wall of the trench, men of strong stature, confident in their speech and physical manner. Ahead of the men lay the bodies of the dead. The two soldiers stopped for a moment, they seemed to be looking for someone, checked each one, and began moving off. They had not even noticed him; how could they not see him? They were not more than two steps past his place of hiding when his body launched like an arrow from a bow.

The man on the right, as they moved slowly side by side, was talking about something they both seemed interested in. He carried his rifle in a relaxed position in his left hand. The other man, who seemed to be listening to his companion's conversation, carried his rifle slung over his right shoulder. He slammed hard into the man on the right, knocking him against his companion pinning both weapons tightly between the two. It was such a shock and surprise that they both lost their balance. As he hit the soldier on the right, using his body to pin the soldier's free arm against his side, the predator's clean left hand went straight to the right side of the head, fingers locking on the eyes and nose, pushing the head away and exposing the neck. With a blurred movement, almost like a muddy bolt of lightening the knife entered in the front of the neck and the blade was swiftly pushed around to the left ear.

All the while the predator kept forcing its prey lower and lower into the bottom of the trench. As the soldier on the left realized what was happening, the blade had moved from his companion's throat and the blunt end of its handle had struck the other soldier in the temple on the right side of his head in one smooth effort. This was not enough to make him unconscious, but caused him to close his eyes and force the soldier to raise his head to open his breathing passage to gather air for his panicking system.

This was the last breath he ever took, for after the handle of the predator's knife left the temple area of the soldier's head, it seemed to automatically know it had created an opening for the blade to strike once again in the neck, and it did with great swiftness. Immediately the predator moved back into his muddy pocket in the side of the trench. Trying to breathe calmly and let the adrenaline take its course, things were better once the shaking and aftereffects of the rush subsided. What just happened? The question screamed through his mind.

Who or what have I become?

This act of violence had only taken a few seconds, yet as he relived it in his mind it seemed forever a dark eternity.

He waited in that very spot, surrounded by death, covered in mud. The desire to sleep was growing, but he knew he could not, not until the dark, and then he would make for safe ground. As darkness came, he listened for several minutes for any sound that seemed out of place. Not detecting anything, he quietly eased up over the lip of the trench and began crawling on his belly toward the tree line in the distance. In the trees, he would still have to be cautious, but the forest would provide ample cover for him to work his way back to the hideaway to share information and reorganize with the others.

As he made his way through the forest, he was thinking how good it would feel to bathe and eat some food, warm or not, maybe some hot coffee or tea. After a short journey, up ahead through an opening in the trees he saw the silhouette of the old farmhouse and the small barn off to the side. He waited for several minutes at the edge of the forest, then made his way slowly to the barn. He found a hole near the old hay pile to one side of the barn. He moved a small portion of the hay, stacked it, and removed a wooden cover that was hidden with dirt and grass. After crawling into the hole, he slid the cover back into place.

The stacked hay fell back over the hidden door. Making his way down a short ladder he entered a tunnel where he could smell food and feel air warmer than the open air above.

After making a couple of turns in the tunnel he entered into a lighted room that was empty. He said the words, "Mary had a little lamb."

"With fleece as white as snow," came a reply from a hidden voice.

Then others came out into the open cavern under the barn. The barn used to be a mill with a water wheel. The cavern was part of the underground stream that supported the use of the wheel and mill. Once the stream dried up the mill was converted to a storage barn, only these few knew of this place under the barn.

Here, this small band could clean up, rest, eat, and plan their resistance efforts against the enemy. When he stepped into the full light of the lanterns that were burning the others gasped, and then they started to laugh softly. Many times they had tested the amount of noise and light they could allow in the cavern without being detected. Smoke from cooking was always filtered further down into the cavern.

One of them could not keep from laughing. Finally, they said, "Look at yourself."

They brought out the old mirror from the farmhouse, a small hand-held mirror they used for signaling and painting their faces to better conceal themselves at night. He gasped when he saw himself. Then he realized why the soldiers in the trench had not noticed him, he looked like a scarecrow made of mud and straw, mostly mud. His eyes and the palm of his left hand were the only white showing, even his teeth looked dirty. He smiled and went off to clean up and change his clothes. Whoever stayed behind always had fresh food, and clean dry clothing ready for when the others returned.

Later when they all were sitting around the table eating and comparing information, they began to relax a little. They each talked of their separate missions, weapons they used, and some of the weapons they had taken from the enemy. He quietly sat, not saying much, just enough to be in the conversation, while cleaning and sharpening his two knives. A couple of the others humorously teased him about his tools of trade. They were not the heavy bladed bone breakers the others carried. They were smaller, yet very strong blades made of fine steel that held a sharp edge very well.

A new member of the group used to work for a shoemaker before the war. He told the others those two blades were knives shoemakers used to cut the old soles off shoes or boots that needed repair, and that was why the steel was so good.

The old members of the group already knew this, for they were there in the beginning. They had watched as he modified the handles, made them a little longer and heavier in case he needed to use a striking action with a blunt object, as he did today.

The third blade he carried was usually always clean, of medium weight, and wrapped with a leather handle. It was used for throwing to cripple or distract an enemy if needed. The story told of the knives being from a shoemaker made him stop and think of his life before this, how he had been just that, making boots and shoes for the nearby provinces and villages where he was from.

Then the violence came and took that from him; and even more, for he had married at an early age. She was a beautiful woman, with hair of long waves of amber curls, and gray-green eyes. They had a young daughter who looked like him, but had her mother's hair. They all had gone to the village that day. His wife and daughter had accompanied him on his business trip to the village, picking up leather and threads. They had wanted to come, so they were all enjoying the day, dining at the outdoor restaurant. He and his wife were having tea. They laughed as their daughter tried to eat the frosting from a very large cookie before the sweet covering melted.

He remembered how wonderful it was, how his wife looked with the light breeze moving her hair across her face partially hiding her eyes. He felt the softness of her lips as she kissed him on the cheek and thanked him for bringing them on his trip to village. Their daughter was giggling and trying to lick her fingers clean of all the sweet covering that had come from the cookie.

Suddenly.

"What is that whistling noise?"

That was the last thing he could remember of them. The shells came from over a mile away and fell upon the village for what seemed liked hours. No one knew that it was coming, they all had heard of the political unrest between the countries but it had always been resolved in the past. There had been no warning.

When he had awakened he was in an old school building that had been changed into a makeshift hospital. His face was bandaged and his right arm had been broken, the rest was minor.

He tried to find out about his wife and daughter but no one could answer his questions.

Eventually he began to get up and move around, looking and asking everywhere. He was told that his wife and daughter had been killed. They must have been; no one had seen them. He was one of the few survivors of the attack. He had been picked up before the enemy soldiers had overrun the village, and had been there in the area of the hospital for three months now. He had noticed a few of the others watching him. They saw he was healing quickly and that he was strong for his size and quick with his hands.

One evening they approached him with the idea that he should join them in their cause. There were seven of them of various ages and backgrounds. They told him they would give him a few days to decide, for their cause was resistance against the enemy, to help free their country and to inflict as much death and destruction on the enemy as possible. As the seven turned to walk away, he was sitting and looking lost, as if he did not even belong in this place let alone this world.

Suddenly, he said, "I will do it."

They turned, and the person they were seeing now was different, as if something had possessed him in the brief moment of silence.

He spoke again, this time so they could hear him clearly, "I will go with you, but first I must return to my home to see what remains, pick up some tools that may be very useful."

They noticed a gleam of light and shadow dance in his eyes. There was a new flame that seemed to fuel his very existence.

The next morning he left with them. They went to his home and place of work, though very little was left at either place. They gathered the little remaining food and other useful items. As they were ready to leave, he kept searching and searching. They urged him to come before the soldiers returned as they would question them as to why they were there.

Finally, under a fallen cabinet, covered in dirt and splinters of wood, he pulled out a small canvas roll, tied with a leather thong. He untied the strap and unrolled the canvas parcel. His search was over, for in this were the tools of the shoemaker, the tools that had helped people from all walks of life. Tools to create and fix shoes and boots for others so they could move with comfort about their lives. Now these tools would be changed, their uses would be much darker than creating comfort, for now they would create mayhem and even death. His eyes glowed; he had a strange smile upon his lips. He stepped out from the wreckage of this former life and said, "Now I am ready."

The others looked at each other in surprise; they knew they had found someone whom they could count on. Now there were eight. They moved off with a determined and quickened pace.

Back in the cavern under the barn, the table was cleared of food and drink. Everything was stored away as if no one had been there; this was done in case they needed to make a sudden exit. Weapons were cleaned, sharpened, and put away; but never out of reach of the one who would use them. Maps were brought out and laid upon the table. Then they began planning the next act in their play of chaos and death. Soon they all sat back, made some tea, and placed two guards, which would always rotate every three hours so they could get some rest. He had first chance to sleep and sleep he did, entering into the sweet darkness without hesitation.

As he awakened, the next mission was more involved, but it was only going to require three of them. The shoemaker was one of the three picked. They were to take out a listening post the enemy had hidden on a hilltop about seven miles from their safe house. They each gathered small amounts of bread and cheese, which would have to last for days if they became separated or injured. Two carried rifles, and old crossbows for the silent work; he carried his knives, and a pistol for backup. Leaving at dusk was their best opportunity to cover the most ground, for they should be near the enemy post by daylight. They would spend a day watching the enemy's activities, counting personnel, and planning methods of approach and attack. They would remain concealed until the night of the second day, then they would take out the listening post and be back in two more days, adding an extra day for slow and concealed travel back to their safe house. The remaining five members would restock the cavern with wood, food, and anything else they could scavenge from the surrounding area.

The ringing of the phone brought him back to his shop of the present. He was still sitting in the wooden chair in front of the patcher, the name given to a sewing machine used to do leather work such as coat repair, sewing torn areas on shoes and boots, putting zippers in bags, or other light leatherwork. This machine could be used for many applications. His was a German-made machine called an Adler; it was roughly thirty years old and worked quite well. Finally realizing where he was, he got up and fell, his legs had no feeling, they had gone numb from sitting in the chair for so long. The phone quit ringing just as he was standing back up. Just as well he thought, he did not want to talk to anyone anyway. He slowly walked over to where he could see the clock; it was late, this time he had been gone for three hours. These occurrences were getting longer and more involved and they were affecting him emotionally and draining him physically.

He decided to stay and catch up on all his work, with that done, he could take some time away. When he finally finished the remaining work, it was nearly sunrise. He left a note for the others who worked there selling footwear, telling them he needed to be gone for a few days. He left the time of his departure and the date of his return. If he would return at all, he thought to himself. Driving home, he began to shed the layers of tension that had built over the course of the day.

What was the purpose for all those people asking him questions? Were they the catalyst behind these visions? On the other hand, was it something deeper within himself, within his psyche, triggering these events to reveal something he was subconsciously seeking?

Entering town, he thought to go by the post office before going home. The sun was above the horizon as he walked out of the post office door. He had a few bills and a small package he would open later at home, for now his body was giving way to its exhaustion and he wanted to be home.

Upon arriving at his small house, he kicked off his shoes and put away the coat and leather bag he carried daily to work. He opened the mail and sorted it, putting the bills in his file to be paid, throwing out the rest, and sat down with the box. He was going to wait, but it seemed to draw him in. It was from his sister and brother-in-law.

After removing the tape that bound the box together for shipping, his hands opened the flap of the box and pulled out the packing paper inside. There among all the packing was a teapot, a small teapot of the most beautiful and exquisite design. Lifting the teapot from the box, he could feel the energy radiating from the pot into his hands.

A calming feeling came over him and he sat down on the large pillows he used as furniture. Silence and darkness soon overcame him like a fog setting on a forest after a hard rain on a summer's day. This time, without hesitation, he went with the feeling.

Mentally letting go, his body slowly relaxed into the pillows. The teapot slid slowly from his hands to an upright position on the floor.

"Would you like some tea?"

He heard a female voice, calm and gentle. The hands holding the teapot were very slender, almost delicate, subtle strength revealed itself in the refined movements of the hands. He replied that he would and thanked her.

A cool breeze was moving the canvas awnings above the stools and small tables where he was sitting. He felt a chill in his body as the breeze moved through his damp clothing. He had been traveling on the open road when the rain began, as he was entering this small farm community.

The woman added the hot water to the fresh cup that was sitting before her. She stopped pouring the steaming water before it was even with the top of the cup, and set the teapot on a small metal frame kept over a source of heat. The teapot caught his eye, its design was very plain, and the color was an earth tone, very subdued. It had no brilliant brushwork or ornate carvings. He could see an inscription of some sort on one side of the pot but from where he sat, he could not make out the meaning. It was beautiful nonetheless, he thought to himself, almost more attractive because of its simple design.

His eyes turned back to the woman's actions. Her motion was effortless and very precise, no obvious waste of energy. She picked up a whisk and lightly churned the tea leaves that had been placed into the cup before the steaming water had been added. When the whisking provided froth, she gracefully set down the whisk in what seemed to be its designated place. Slowly she picked up the cup by lightly grasping the sides with one hand, one palm up underneath, pointing toward the customer. She gestured for him to take the cup as she presented it.

Taking the cup as she suggested, he held onto the sides with one hand, for there was no handle, and placed the other hand under the cup, letting it sit in the palm of his hand.

"Now, feel what the herbs and steaming water have to offer before you drink it down," she said with a smile.

The fragrance from the tea filled his sense of smell and unconsciously he began to smile. His smile revealed to her that the spirit of the tea had indeed accomplished the intention. "Please enjoy the taste of the tea and feel its warmth as it enters the inner realm of the body," she said.

By doing this, he noticed how the chill slowly left his body and the fragrance provided some sort of uplifting energy.

The street that ran through the length of the village was lined with shops. It was late evening and the street was dimly lit with lighting coming from the various shops along each side. The road was not of dirt but a type of small round stones that provided a solid base for the carts and foot travel that frequented the area. The small stones reflected the light from the shops as the rainwater ran lightly around them giving the impression that one was sitting by a small stream and not in the middle of a village. The shops were all busy despite the wet conditions. The shops with the awnings provided the effect of branches and leaves of large trees lining each side of the bank of a flowing stream.

The fog and light rain kept the different smells from the shops close to the ground as if not wanting to share such a variety of sweet odors with the heavens above. After he finished a second cup of tea he felt much better and realized he was hungry. He asked if she served any food.

"It is late but I have some fish and some vegetables and fruit left," she replied.

"I do not want to keep you," he said.

"No, no—I meant that is what I have left this late in the day. I will not close for two more hours."

"I will take a serving of whatever you have."

As she prepared his order, the rain stopped. The moon made its way from behind the parting clouds. They shared conversation covering a variety of topics. The conversation revealed they had much in common and both had been travelers at different times in their lives. Actually, they had been to some of the same places.

Once the food was ready, she set it in front of him and noticed he bowed his head and said some quiet words. Must be a prayer of thanks she thought to herself as she busied herself with cleaning and organizing the little shop before she would close. He ate slowly, enjoying the meal; the vegetables and fruit were surprisingly fresh. He thanked her and asked for the charge. She said it was on her; it was not often she had the opportunity to visit with someone who had shared many of the same travels and interests as she had.

He thanked her and told her he could not totally accept the free meal; however, he would like to help her clean up so she could close on time. She smiled and said that she accepted the offer.

Once he got behind the counter he unrolled one of his leather cases he was carrying. It was lined with different knives and other cutlery. He took out two knives and a large ladle with a fancy twisted handle. She was surprised at his collection.

"Those are very nice, where did you get them?" she asked.

Before answering he smiled, then said, "These are for you. I noticed when you were cutting the vegetables your knives were not cutting very well. Now you can use less effort and accomplish more. This ladle will help with your soups and other fruit dishes. To answer your question, I make these. That is what I do. Please tell me your name. If you prefer not to, just give me the first initials to your first and last name."

She did not hesitate as he thought she might, she told him her name. He took out another tool from a different section of the leather case.

He quickly sat down and carved her initials in each of the items. He put his tools away, rolled up the case and began helping with the clean up. She watched him for a while, unsure of what and who this stranger was. She had never seen a stranger so at ease with himself in what he was doing. She watched him closely as he helped her clean and prepare for the next day. She washed the new knives and ladle. She handled the knives several times, there was something about them, and they seemed to fit her, to adjust to her hands perfectly.

He watched her closely as they worked together; he was amazed at her grace. She moved effortlessly he thought, no wasted movements, her eyes had a gleam as if they held and kept a hidden secret of spiritual importance. He smiled to himself as he watched her handle the knives. She even pulled out some whole vegetables and chopped them up for the next day just to see how the blades would cut. When she looked up at him, she was smiling.

He spoke first. "You can't keep handling them," he laughed, "or you will wear them out the first day."

She laughed and replied, "I just can't seem to let go of them. I am taking them to show my father. We have a small farm close to here. In fact, that is where all these fruits and vegetables come from. We grow them ourselves."

He was impressed with how hard she seemed to work; yet, there was still an air of excitement and enjoyment as she continued her chores. When they finished the cleaning, it was time for her to close. He thanked her for the meal, picked up all the leather cases and packed. He took one quick look at her, a look where he completely engaged her eyes and energy. She shivered.

"Thank you for everything," he said. "It was truly my privilege to have the opportunity to meet and speak with someone like you. I enjoyed it."

He turned swiftly, and was gone before she could respond.

She just stood there. Why had she not spoken, she could have said something, but no, like a mute, she watched as he walked away. She locked up her shop and began the walk home to her father's farm. She greeted the other shop owners as they, too, began closing their places of business. They all knew each other, it was a small community; friendly and close knit. The farm was located on the outskirts of the village, about a half-mile walk from the shop. In fact, the village was surrounded on all sides with small farms and orchards.

The moon finally revealed itself from the clouds and lighted her way. As she approached the farmhouse she could see her father patiently sitting on the porch, as he always did, waiting for her return. His wife was sitting next to him doing some sort of needlework, and chatting with her father. Her father, sitting quietly, smoking his pipe and listening to her mother, tried to look surprised when she came close to the front of the house. She knew he could see clearly to the edge of the village and that he always knew when she was returning.

He greeted her warmly as did her mother, putting down her work.

The young woman sat down on the step of the porch and began telling of the pleasant stranger who had come into the shop to have tea during the rain. She told how they had shared conversation and he had finally decided to eat. She told them that the stranger helped her clean up and gave her two new knives and a ladle to use at the shop as payment for the food.

"Did you bring them with you?" her father asked.

"Yes, I wanted to show you, they are very special, something different about them."

She pulled them from her bag. She had wrapped them in a waxed cloth to carry them home. She handed them one by one to her father as she unwrapped them.

The ladle was first. He admired the work and commented on the skill of the craftsman

"Did you ask the stranger where he had gotten them?" her father asked.

"Oh, he said that he makes them himself, that is what he does for work, his trade craft," his daughter replied with a proud tone in her voice. Her father looked at her for a moment, then his eyes saw the initials.

"How does he know your name?"

"I told him," she replied. "Then he put the initials in as I watched."

"You saw him do this?" her father asked in a surprised voice.

"Yes."

"May I see the knives?" her father asked.

As she carefully handed the knives to him she said, "Be careful, they are very sharp."

As soon as he touched them, he gasped, he just stared at the two well-made blades, then he saw the initials again.

"And you say you saw the man put the initials in these also?"

"Yes."

There was a small stump about ten feet in front of the porch used for last minute things, chopping extra wood, cleaning tools, or pounding and straightening tools and handles for his fields and garden work. He took one knife, flipped it in his hand, and threw it at the stump. There was a clean solid sound as it sank deep into the wood. He picked up another knife, threw it, and it landed next to the first knife he had thrown. His daughter was shocked.

"Why did you do that and how did you know how to do that?"

He just looked at his daughter and walked off the porch to retrieve the knives.

The young woman, somewhat stunned, looked at her mother, who quietly spoke.

"Your father has not always been a farmer."

She added, "He was a soldier before we were married, and a skilled one at that."

The man came back and sat down next to his daughter, handing her back her .gifts. He looked straight at her and asked, "Was this stranger older, like me?"

"No," she replied. "He was closer to my age."

"Really," her father replied, looking bewildered at his daughter's answer.

"Yes," she said, "and when he finished helping me, he picked up his things, thanked me, and quickly walked away."

"Did you get a name?" her father asked.

"No," she replied. "That is just it; he disappeared so quickly I did not even think to ask it."

Then her father smiled. "It must be his son," was all he said, as he stood and stared toward the village.

"You know you were followed part way here tonight," her father said.

"No," she replied.

The mother gasped. "You saw this and did nothing," she proclaimed.

Her husband turned and looked at them both. "It was the same two boys from the other village that come here to drink and try to find some new girls."

"Why didn't you do something about it if you knew it?" his wife asked.

He replied, "I was preparing to walk that way when I saw a figure rise up out of our field, from no where. I was startled, and very swiftly the figure put down the two boys and disappeared into the field. That is what I was watching intently when you came up to the porch. You see, the two boys were just getting up. I know of the two boys, they are harmless; they are more of a threat to each other when they are drinking. However, obviously your guardian from the shadows did not know that. I doubt though if he hurt them very much. I will walk you into the shop in the morning and see if there are any stories of excitement from this night."

The father looked directly at his daughter.

"Did you hear anything behind you, anything at all?" he asked.

"Well," she responded, looking puzzled. "I thought I heard some voices, but when I turned onto our path I looked back and there was nothing there."

"I watched, as I do every night; I know you know I watch you come home. Tonight I was going down to talk to those two young men when that figure appeared, disposed of them, and slipped back into the field. It stunned me to see this; it made me realize how complacent I may have become, or maybe too trusting and comfortable living like this." He turned and looked at his wife and then his daughter.

He was very quiet for a moment, then said with a tone of warm tenderness, "I love you both so very much, and you have brought happiness and meaning to my existence. I have seen so much that was cruel and ugly in my early years that I guess I felt it was all behind me and only good things would come. However, when I saw the figure rise out of our own field it awakened all of my past senses. I will say this with all certainty, once the two young men went down I felt a peace, as if someone was watching over you and was as concerned as I was. I just do not know how, whoever that was, even got into that place in our field without me seeing him or frightening the birds that always flock there. Do not ask me to explain, but I know there is no threat to us from that person. It would seem my daughter, that you have, at least for one night, acquired a guardian shadow."

Slowly she rose, holding on tightly to her gifts wrapped in the cloth. Slowly she walked out to the stump and stared into the darkness.

The next morning was cool and the clouds had moved on with the wind. The morning sun was heating up the damp earth and causing steam to rise from the planted fields that surrounded the village.

The daughter rose quickly and began her morning duties on the farm. As she came around the house from the barn she noticed her father out in the field near the road where she walked to and from work in the village. He appeared to be looking for something. Her mother came out onto the porch and banged on an empty pan. Her husband turned toward the house and waved his arm, letting his wife know he had acknowledged her and would be in for the morning meal.

As the mother turned to go back in, she looked at her daughter, with a smile on her face she said, "Your father is going to be different to you. This stranger has awakened in him a new energy along with his curiosity for something new. Be patient with him, it will be good for him. But around you he will be different. I have not seen him like this for many years. When he stopped being a soldier and his farming began to become too familiar, I began to see him slip away from the man I once knew. I feel this is good, but be patient, for he will now be in your hair." She laughed, "That means he won't be in mine." She laughed again and said, "Come in and eat."

As she went into the house she said to her daughter,

"You now have a new companion whether you want one or not."

It seemed this event with the stranger at the shop had brought on a new energy for everyone in the household. Even the mother seemed happier, and her daughter thought it was probably due to her father getting out of her space with his constant new ideas and conversations, usually distracting the mother from her moments of peace during the day.

When her father walked in from the field, he cleaned himself off at the door, slipped out of his boots and into his house shoes. They all sat down at the table, said a prayer of thanks, and began the morning meal. The mother asked her husband what he was doing out in that section of the field. She was hiding a smile as she engaged in the conversation, but her daughter could not help but notice the twinkle of delight dancing in her eyes almost as if she were keeping a secret from everyone.

He replied, "I was looking at the crops along the road, seeing if they were getting enough water."

He looked directly at his wife. She couldn't contain it any longer; a laugh burst from her, and she said, "You just could not stand it, could you? You are like a boy that has ventured upon something so mysterious that you have to investigate everything."

His face flushed, "All right all right," he said. "I was trying to see if there was any trace of the person's presence last night. When I went to look where I believed the stranger had entered and waited for the two young men, I found no tracks, no sign at all."

She put on a face of concern, falsely, but convincing if you did not know her, and said, "This may need much more investigation my love."

Then he looked at her and replied, "Oh, just eat woman, you know nothing of these matters."

Then they both were laughing, to their daughter's amazement. They always seemed to have some secret communication pertaining to life and love in their relationship. They always seemed to know the hidden intentions of the other, whether it was masked to an outsider or not. He then turned with a serious look on his face, and spoke to his daughter.

"I believe I should accompany you for a couple of days to and from work."

Her mother agreed, also with a great tone of concern, which drew a quick smile from her father.

It was a game to them; they both had involved themselves in her activities as if it was a new and exciting game.

Nevertheless, she knew from experience there would be no challenging these ideas because they both agreed, even if it was for different reasons.

After finishing her meal, she cleaned up everything and prepared to leave for work. She slipped out the back, hoping to avoid her father's new idea for adventure.

He called from the shadow of the house, "Are you ready?" as if it was normal for him to be there. He knew she would try to slip off, but he acted as if everything was going as planned.

They began the walk into the village, greeting other travelers and workers along the way. She noticed his stride was far livelier, lighter than normal. As he greeted each person his eyes would take in the whole person as if he could see differently than before. She had never seen him like this; this could prove to be interesting she thought, learning something of him she had never known before, although she had heard stories of him as a young man. She remembered them as tales used to keep children in line or to display a little more respect toward their elders, especially the parents.

As they entered the village, the activities were well underway for the new day. Many shops would open before hers. She opened early enough for people to visit her for the mid-day meal, and they could have tea and fruit drinks and some food up to and through the evening meal. A group of farmers gathered off to one side, talking excitedly and comparing tools. She and her father walked over to the farmers.

The farmers greeted them. The people were always eager to share new ideas and events of the community. One farmer showed them the new tip for his hoe, how sharp and well made it was. Others had various tools, from carving knives and small rake heads to sickles. The farmers were most impressed that each one of their new tools had their own personal mark or initials on it. A woman even had a small set of spoons for her kitchen and needles for sewing.

Her father asked where they had purchased these items, and they told him of the young man passing through the village that morning.

"Where did he go?" he asked. "I wonder if he can repair broken tools."

The other farmers said they believed he could, according to his conversation with them, but he had left.

"He is gone?" The daughter blurted out, surprising everyone, including herself.

"Yes," one of the farmers said. "He said he had to deliver tools to another village. We asked if he would come back this way but he said it was not likely, he had far to go and that it would be out of his way to return. His destination lay in another province and he needed to be there with their tools; he was very kind and seemed a skilled craftsman, but very determined to get on his journey. He said some day he may come this way again because the people were so kind and seemed interested in his work. He had not traveled this way before."

The daughter recovered from her outburst and hid her disappointment by saying, "Oh, I was hoping to get a few more items for my shop. I had gotten some nice things from him last night when he ate his evening meal."

A woman from a shop next to the daughter's came walking up to the group. She said she had to return home shortly to take her husband a new tool she had gotten from the traveler. She handed the daughter a letter and said the traveler had left it with her to give to the young woman for the kindness of the tea and meal at the last moment. Then the woman handed the father a small box.

"What is this?" he asked.

"I don't know, but the traveler said to give it to you. He rewarded me for this action so I must honor his request by giving it to you personally."

"What do you mean?" he asked.

"He gave me very sharp needles to sew with, this beautiful pin to wear, and a new sickle for my husband to harvest the crops with, if I personally handed the box to you. I told him it would be done. Now I must hurry home, as I have someone watching my shop until my return."

The woman turned and quickly walked away. The group of farmers began to break up, for they all had work to do and they were anxious to try out their new tools.

The father said to his daughter, "Let us go also, you have to get your shop ready to open." They both looked strangely at one other and walked in silence to the location of her shop. She unlocked the side door to the small place and they stepped inside. She put down her things and hung up her jacket.

"Before you open up, let us see what this mysterious person has left, as clues," her father said.

So she opened her letter and began reading.

Dear friend,

May I think of you as a new friend? Your kindness to me last evening overwhelmed me. I so enjoyed your company and conversation that I was sorry that I had to leave so soon. It is not often I meet one as open in thought and as willing to share with a stranger. You have made me feel as if I may have found a new friend, but duties call me away. Life's needs and requirements pull us in many directions, often times they require us to attend to matters we would rather put off, or maybe realize that they are not that important at all. However, I have given my word and without it I am nothing, so I must continue my journey. I know not if I will ever see you again, I feel that I may not. It was of strange reasons I traveled this route this time. Your father will explain this to you. But know if God does not allow us to ever share another smile, a cup of tea, or even another word, I hold you in a special place of its own in my heart. Your beauty and grace also overwhelmed me. I felt my heart willing to betray me, at the glance of your eyes or the presence of your smile. Your hands moving gracefully among their duties were of perfect action. I feel if I stayed another day, I would lose my focus on my business at hand. I do not wish to incur any unnecessary attention from your father. I have heard of this man, this warrior turned farmer. All things aside, the beauty of your being, and its actions and non-actions, I found affected me greatly. Know that you will always be honored with good thoughts.

So long my new friend. I pray your life is as beautiful as you are.

The young woman's hands dropped to her sides, one held the letter; a tightness appeared in her stomach and moved up to her throat. She could not speak; all she could do was wave her free hand in a foolish gesture.

Her father opened the box that had been given to him. As he lifted the lid off the box, he saw a very fine cloth covering an object. Upon removing the cloth, a knife, a most beautiful knife, was revealed. The blade was seven inches in length, polished to a mirror-like finish, and had a cloud pattern design on the cutting edge of the blade. The handle was four and one-half inches long, smoothly sanded, and lacquered.

In addition, to his surprise, his crest was embedded in the exotic wood of the handle. The crest was made of precious metals. The scabbard that held the blade was of the same wood as the handle, polished and lacquered to a very high finish, and engraved with his initials. The knife was simple, in perfect balance, and could be worn daily and used for many things; yet was so beautifully done that it represented great care from the craftsman to the bearer of this tool or weapon.

The daughter noticed that as her father handled the knife there seemed to be something taking place between him and the blade. It moved from hand to hand, and seemed so balanced that he was losing himself in the action of handling the knife itself.

Removed from the shock of her letter, she became mesmerized by the actions of her father as he gracefully moved around the inside of the shop. He dodged obstacles in slow motion; the blade seemed to guide his body through thrusts and blocks disguised as a dance. She never knew he could be so focused, so graceful, and yet quick and light on his feet; however, there was one time when she and her father were working in the garden and they heard a noise from the house as if her mother had fallen. By the time she realized what might have happened, her father was entering the door some fifty paces away.

She always wanted to ask him how he had accomplished such a feat. Now she knew there was so much more to him than just his annoying humor and constant urging for her to become better and better at what she chose to pursue. Some of what he did show her was the use of the staff and the knife for basic protection; but she excelled in the art of the bow and arrow. She seemed to connect with the weapon as an extension of her soul. Often she would practice when the summer brought the extended light to the evening. Then he would praise her proficiency or criticize her for her careless approach to the ancient art when she was not focused.

He continued to move faster and faster without concern for the closed in surrounding. His hands seemed to dart in and around things at lightning speed while holding the knife with such ease. Then without warning, he stopped as if it all had completed something hidden inside of him. Beads of sweat had gathered on his face, but a smile seemed to reveal the pure joy he felt during the action. He wiped the blade with a special movement and placed it back in the scabbard. He did not place the knife back into the box but fixed it carefully on a sash around his waist that he used like a belt.

As he began to close the lid on the box, he saw another cloth with something obviously wrapped in it. Slowly he took the cloth and unwrapped it. There in his hand was a hand-braided cord with a strange but beautifully designed pendant. A circle of silver and wood, and enclosed within the circle was the outline or shape of a heart made of gold. Inside the cloth lay another letter. He wrapped the pendant back up and placed it in the box, pulled out the letter, unfolded it, and began to read the contents. All the while, the young woman was amazed at her father's newly displayed skills and focus. However, as she saw his demeanor change she began getting things ready to open the shop.

She felt it would be better if she allowed him to read his letter before she told him about hers. This truly was a strange event in their lives, she thought as she opened the doors and cleaned the awning of the dust that had gathered after the rain. Her father began reading his letter from the stranger—it captivated him immediately.

Sir,

    Please forgive my unannounced intrusion into your life and that of your family. The night I came in out of the rainstorm to get a cup of tea, I was taken by the beauty and mannerisms of the young woman who was attending to my tea and food. I could readily see that she had received some type of disciplined training sometime in her life. Then I noticed her bag that she must carry to and from work, and how a certain metal pin, a warrior's crest, was placed on the bag. The crest I recognized because my father spoke many times of it and of the honorable man to whom the crest belonged. I realized the lovely woman who ran the shop must be your daughter. My father heard you may be living in this area and asked me to make contact with you to deliver a gift from him: the knife he taught me to make. He has passed his skills of craftsmanship on to me through the years. He and my mother live in the province three days journey from here. He always said he hoped to see you again one day. That should clear up many of your questions. I hope this helps with the rest. Last night when I had tea and my meal here, I gave your daughter some gifts for her and her shop. Also, after observing her I knew she would show you and you would come to understand your old acquaintance was still of this world.

As I left the shop, I heard two young men talking about the beauty of your daughter, and saying she was not attached to anyone. I could tell they had much to drink; they thought they would approach her and see if they could steal a kiss from her. I do not believe they meant to do any real harm, but not knowing them at all, I felt it would not be correct of me to leave such matters to fate. As I followed them I overhead one of them say that it was not a good idea because of the stories he had heard of her father. That gave me an idea, so I put the plan into effect. I hid my belongings and followed your daughter to the edge of your farm. It was then I saw you sitting on the porch of your home, a distance away. I knew it was you casually watching for your daughter. She may not even be aware that is the reason you sit as you do in the evening. I knew you would see me immediately once the moon came out from the moving clouds, so I waited for the next cloud to hide the light of the moon.

It was then that I slipped into your field, crawling in between the rows of plants. It was there I waited for your daughter to pass and then I knew the two young men would soon follow because they would be running out of opportunity. As they approached my position, another cloud hid the light of the moon, allowing me to be even more effective. I did not wish to hurt them, just rough them up a little and scare them. After both were knocked down on the road rather hard, I said in a quiet voice, "Do not follow my daughter anymore, you must address me before addressing her."

I knew this would add more to your reputation and probably keep advances toward her known to you. I removed myself from your field by crawling backwards using my fingers as a rake, removing any trace of my being there. I then advanced close enough to hear your family's conversations, including the concerns of your wife, who I could see you respect very much. This pendant is for her, for I saw that quietly and secretly her heart is at the center of your circle of life. You love her very much. Now I know why my father admired your skills so much. Your willingness to listen to others and evaluate the entire situation before acting is a very rare quality indeed. Most people carry out an action on pure emotion or intellectual reason; or both combined, not allowing the whole picture to present itself. Then they face creating a completely new system of problems that would also need dealing with, including the unnecessary loss of those near and dear to one's self.

At this point, he laughed aloud and began rubbing his chin with his free hand and nodding his head as if he was having a conversation with the person who had penned the letter.

His daughter realized the small burst of laughter was more a sign of understanding something than actually finding a great deal of humor in what was being taken in.

He continued reading his letter.

> *Please forgive me for entering and departing your life in such a manner. I needed to attend to the wishes of my father so I did not leave until I observed the woman hand your daughter the letter, and you, the box.*

"What? He was still here!"

The daughter turned, asking her father, "What did you say?"

"I said he was still here. He watched the woman hand you the letter and hand me the box."

The young woman's shoulders sank, and disappointment overcame her once again. Soon she put aside her emotions and continued working; the customers would soon be coming for mid-day refreshments.

Her father looked around at the street and then continued reading.

After I saw you each had your items, I left your village as I have far to go and much to do. Forgive me for my abruptness.

He had a smile growing on his face; he had come to admire the young man, just from his actions and from the letter.

I do not travel this area because it takes me off my route by a great distance. I may not return this way again. I have put information at the bottom on how to communicate with my father. He would truly enjoy hearing from you, as he said, he hopes to see his old friend again. Please give this pendant to your wife and explain to her these events. I will wave to her if she is out when I pass. Ask her if she noticed a stranger waving at her, carrying a large load, and moving at a good pace on the main road.

I pray you all stay well and that God provides a smooth path for you to walk on and a cool breeze for your evenings on the porch.

The letter ended with information about how to reach his old friend. He folded the letter, put it back in the box with the pendant and tucked it inside his jacket.

Seeing a strange melancholy expression on her face, he turned to his daughter. "I see that your letter brings disappointment to you."

She looked up. He could see she was fighting to keep her voice steady, holding back emotion, portraying strength and control.

"Yes," she said stoically. "I was hoping to see him again, maybe purchase a few more utensils for the shop. They are so well made."

Then she turned away. He did not pursue the conversation. He allowed her to keep herself together for the incoming customers. He asked her if she would like him to stay around and help with anything. As she turned, he saw tears being wiped away. She said no, that she would be fine. He gave her a quick hug and moved off without any more conversation. He lingered in the village for a while, bought some cakes to take home for his wife; she always loved them with tea. He visited with different people and moved off toward the small farm. I will give the pendant and the letter to my wife as we have the cakes and tea, he thought to himself. That should help her from being totally focused on what she knew would be disappointing to her daughter. Also, for me being back in her hair sooner than she would have hoped for, he said to himself, laughing.

Arriving at the farm, he went around, entering the house from the back. His wife was singing as she worked in the garden, hoeing or cleaning the rows between plants, and bending every now and then to pick a *renegade weed*, as she called them. She had such a connection to all things of life, and her movements were always graceful. He could see what the stranger had been speaking of when he said that his wife was the heart of his circle of life. Suddenly she looked up.

"What is wrong? Why are you back so soon?" She asked urgently.

"I am sorry that you feel that way toward me," he said with a smile. "I know you expected more time to yourself, but I have something for you, and a treat. Since my presence disrupts you so, I will leave you alone."

He knew she loved surprises.

"What do you mean you have a treat and something for me?" she asked.

She moved toward him and leaned the hoe against the post of the gate to the garden.

"I think we should sit down in the shade of the porch and have some tea and cakes," he told her. "I bought them for you, but I thought I would also like to share one with you."

"Oh, you would, would you?" she replied with a smile. "I was just enjoying the sun, can it wait?"

Then he handed her the box, but as he moved his arm, the knife fastened to his side was revealed.

"Where did you get that?" she asked, as she pointed at the knife.

"Please," he said, "let us just sit and have the tea and cakes. There is something in the box for you, and I have a letter explaining it all. Then I promise I will get out of your hair."

She turned, looking surprised, "You will?"

"Yes," he responded, "Please sit. I will make the tea and bring the cakes."

Sitting down, she thought, this is really turning out to be a strange day. Then she looked at her husband and smiled to herself. She would not question this special treatment; she would play along as long as she could.

"By the way," she said, as he brought out the tea and cakes, "I was moving around to the side of the house this morning to get the hoe and someone was waving heartily at me from the road. I thought it may be one of our neighbors, but then I realized he was moving too fast and the load he was carrying was quite large."

Her husband interrupted her. "You had better open the box," he said as he placed a cake in front of her and poured her some tea.

She was truly enjoying this attention. She held the tea, savored the warmth and aroma of the herbs, and took a small sip for it was still quite hot. Then she reached for a cake and was just about to take a bite; she noticed her husband staring at her. The cake dropped from her hand, and she blurted out, "That was him wasn't it? The traveler on the road; was that him who waved at me?"

She sat back in her chair, still staring at her husband.

"There truly is nothing to worry about is there?" she calmly said.

"Please," he said to her, "open the box then read the letter."

Astonished, she said, "Letter?" Carefully she opened the box; she saw that it was also what the knife had been laying in. She removed the cloth wrapped around the pendant, she gasped as she saw it. "How beautiful this is, and what skilled workmanship."

The letter was slowly unfolded. The tea and cakes sat untouched the whole time she read the letter. Tears began to form at the corners of her eyes and then slowly made small shining trails down each check. Upon finishing the letter she looked at her husband and asked, "May I see the knife?"

He took it from his sash and handed it to her in the formal manner, with the handle facing her as she reached for it, demonstrating total trust with the action. She always felt so connected to him when he treated her with such formal respect. She marveled at the knife's balance and craftsmanship. It was indeed a spiritual work, and made very well. In time she handed her husband back the knife and scabbard, which he replaced in the sash.

She then asked him to put the pendant around her neck as she leaned forward. He stood and moved to her side then gently moved her long hair with one hand. He brought the braided cord around and hooked it together, then sat back down and said, "Beautiful—the pendant also. The pendant looks very good on you."

When his wife realized the implication of his statement, she blushed and knew that the stranger's words in the letter were true. Often things like this were taken for granted when people are together for a long time. Words such as those are not often spoken, or they are easily dismissed as teasing. However, she knew and felt all was true.

"Tea and cakes," he blurted out. "They need to be consumed to be enjoyed."

They both laughed in the moment. As they shared the tea and cakes his wife said, "This must have been quite disappointing to our daughter."

"Yes," he said, "but you know her, she is bravely continuing as if nothing happened. You may need to speak with her alone."

His wife sat quietly for awhile; then she looked directly at him and asked, "This stranger is truly a remarkable young man is he not?"

"Yes, more so than both his father and I together."

"Are you going to contact his father," she asked.

"Yes, as soon as possible. Don't you think I should?" he replied.

"Yes definitely, she said. We should get together very soon. I would love to meet him, and his wife."

The days rolled into weeks, the weeks into months. Finally, the parents of the young traveler visited and stayed for a week's time. They were wonderful people. There was still a bond between the two men, the young warriors who both turned to farming and other quiet trades of talent and honor; talents that could serve and benefit the whole. The women became the best of friends. They had many of the same interests and shared their other skills between them. The stranger's parents both admired the daughter and her discipline. There was little talk of the son, but one night the daughter overheard a conversation between her father and his old friend about him, as the two men sat out in the cool night air.

"Have you heard from your son lately?"

"No," the other man replied. "The last I heard he was crafting tools for a temple or monastery in some province. He was trading his work for study about God."

"Will he become one of them?" the young woman's father asked.

"I don't know. It is possible with him. When he was younger, I taught him the ways of the warrior. He was good, very good. His staff and knife skills were beyond comparison. His sword skill was remarkable, but to him it was mainly for killing or maiming a man, even in defense. Early in his life he saw the corruption in the leaders and in government; he also saw the caste system and the power struggles within the military. These both sickened him. He turned from all that I had to offer except the crafting skills. In that trade he is unmatched, and I think it has to do with his love of the work and his spiritual beliefs."

Then the young woman's father told the stranger's father of the night his son met his daughter, how the young man quietly protected her right in front of him, not revealing anything or leaving any evidence that he had even been there.

How he had frightened and roughed up the two young men, but did no real harm to them.

"In fact," he said, "a few weeks later the two young men approached me and apologized. People say they have both become better individuals since then."

Then both fathers laughed.

The stranger's father stopped laughing and said, "I am glad you told me of this; sometimes I wondered if he would actually be able to care for himself."

"For a few weeks, I have been hearing strange stories of a young toolmaker helping people out with rogues and bandits, then disappearing. I know that it is your son, but without the letter he left with your wonderful gift, I would never have known what to do when those two boys came to apologize, for he made a point that they thought it was me."

After hearing the conversation, the daughter began to believe she would never see him again. She was filled with sorrow—she believed they could have been great friends. However, that was a lie, she said to herself. She wanted to be more than that to him, and she wanted him to be much more than that to her. But now?! She went into the garden behind the house and burst into tears.

The two women sitting at the back of the house heard this. The stranger's mother rose to attend to the sound. Gently, the young woman's mother touched her hand and said, "Please just let her be alone, this flood of emotion has been a long time coming, the gates are open now, let it flow as needed."

The other woman sat down and nodded; "Yes, it is probably the best action at this time."

At the week's end, many surprises took place. A farm not far from the daughter and her parents was for sale. The parents of the stranger talked it over and decided to buy it, for the climate and soil was much better than in their present province. They bought the new farm, and packed some things so they could go back and sell their old farm. Both families agreed as to the wonderful possibilities for the future in business and community. With the help of the daughter's family and friends, the stranger's family made the return journey.

They settled in their new farm only a short distance away in a month's time. No one had heard any recent news from the son. The months rolled into a year and another season had passed. The families were getting together often, traveling to festivals and gathering supplies from other provinces and villages. They enjoyed sharing their lives; the good and challenging times.

One day they were visiting another province; both couples were together as the women had accompanied the men to get supplies. While they were eating at a roadside inn, they overheard a story of a young man helping some elderly farmers being robbed on their journey home from a market. The battle was violent but the young man and the farmers prevailed. Most of the bandits were captured or killed. The amazing thing was, not a farmer was hurt, but the young man was injured and they did not know if he even lived.

The couples began asking questions around the village but no one knew much more. It had happened a few months earlier, and had taken place closer to another village; but again, no one knew where to look. After hearing about the young man's injury, the return trip home was a somber one, no one willing to admit that it sounded like the son. But then again, he was supposed to be far from here. Returning home, the daughter saw something different about her parents so she asked what had happened. They told her the story as they had heard it, and said no one knew who the stranger was or where exactly it had taken place. The daughter did not ask any questions, in fact, the only thing she did do was stop talking for the rest of the day.

The following day she completed her work early at the farm. She had much to do at the shop. The seasons were changing and the leaves were beginning to fall. This meant she had to begin gathering things for the coming winter. Different herbs would need to be gathered, more wood stacked, and she would have to begin to clean and store the awnings. She would then paint and hang the shutters. She was organized. When she saw something that needed attention, she would attend to it and do a little bit at a time. She was not one who saved everything to do at the last minute. Besides, this activity would help her to stop thinking of the stranger.

The night before she had said to her mother, "It is time to stop this foolishness of thinking about someone who would never return; especially after the latest story in which he may not be alive. Besides, he stated he probably would not return this way. He is not aware his family has even moved here. Do you know how many markets and festivals I have searched just to glimpse his face? Do you know how many times I hoped the next stranger carrying a load into the village would be him? I am a fool—I did not even know him, but his letter was wonderful, and vague at the same time. So now I begin anew, starting fresh tomorrow, new ideas, new hopes, and new dreams. You will see—I may even make the shop bigger. My life has just taken a change for the better."

And that is how she had ended the night before. Today she was making good on her word.

The young woman's father heard the conversation between mother and daughter the night before and decided to leave himself out of it altogether unless she asked for help at the shop.

The fall day was cold, even though there was much sunshine during the day. The sun set earlier and the evenings were filled with the sweet smell of the wood burning stoves used for heating homes and shops as well as for cooking. She closed her shop earlier in the fall and winter because the travelers and workers did not come as late; no one wanted to be out in the cold after dark. The day had gone well, people came and went and all were excited about the upcoming harvest festival; the last festival before the winter snows came. However, sometimes the snows fooled everyone and came early, just to add spice to their lives, she thought. When the last customer paid and left, she began cleaning and making plans for the next day. Earlier, as she was preparing a meal and talking excitedly with some customers about the harvest festival, she had spilled some herbs that fell below the counter.

As she was bending down below the counter straightening up the herbs, she heard a voice.

"Is it too late for some tea?"

"Yes," she replied without looking up, "I am just closing and almost ready to leave."

"Forgive me. I did not realize it was that late, I am sorry to have troubled you."

The herbs fell from her hands. The voice! How could this be? She quickly rose up and saw the customer with a staff walking away with a slight limp.

Just before he got out of sight into the dim light of the street, she said, "Wait, please wait, I am sorry. I believe I have hot water left in the pot enough for a cup, maybe two. I should not waste it."

Her heart was beating so hard she thought that it might shatter. The customer turned toward her, but stayed in the shadows.

"Thank you for your kindness but I do not wish to keep you. The night will grow cold soon and you must be on your way."

"I could use some help if you have a moment," she cried out.

There was nothing but silence. Could that have been him? Why didn't I look up? Why didn't I look up when he first asked for tea?

Then the figure moved into the light of her shop.

"How may I help you," he asked.

She looked up into the face of the stranger.

 PART TWO

Her mouth dropped open, tears began to build, her voice refused to respond. She could do nothing but stare. He was leaner than before; a cut was healing along the right side of his face above his eye and down around to the cheek. One hand had a leather guard laced over it similar to that of a glove and she could see bandages underneath it. He looked at her for a moment then spoke as he took a step forward.

"You may not remember me," he said, "but..."

"STOP!" she cried out, "STOP, just sit down. I have not

stopped thinking of you all this time; my anger, my sadness, and my feelings for you have almost destroyed me because I could not stop thinking of you. You just left me. You know that? You just left me."

He had yet to sit down. At this outburst, he turned and started limping out of the shop.

"Wait," she said, "I am not through."

He quickly held up his hand and then disappeared. Suddenly he reappeared with a horse loaded with larger packs, and he himself had a large pack. He tied the horse close to the shop, brought his large pack in, and asked if he could set it in the light. He did not trust the darkness in an unknown place. She said that he could. She stared at him in disbelief.

"What? You won't do what again? What do you mean?" she asked.

He looked at her as he limped to the stool and leaned the staff against the counter and sat down. "I won't leave you again," he said. "All of this is everything I own; my tools, my belongings, some crafted things, all of it. I have gathered everything. I have finished my duties and debts, my promises to others. Now I have come back to see if I could find you, to see if you have any interest in me, in us, at all?"

Tears were running down her checks. She turned, poured some water into a bucket and set it out so the horse could drink. She quickly began preparing the tea as she had done on the day she had first seen him more than a year ago. She did not speak, she just moved, the action was working; it was allowing her to relax and compose herself.

She poured the water and whisked the herbs in the cup to a froth. Laying down the whisk, she gracefully picked up the cup and extended it to him.

"Please feel the warmth of the tea and allow the fragrance of the herbs to fill your being before drinking," she said with a smile.

From what seemed like another lifetime he did as she requested, but before he drank, he looked at her and said, "You said you may have enough water in the teapot for two cups, won't you please join me?"

She prepared a second cup and sat down beside him. They both sat and just looked at one another.

Finally she spoke.

"We should drink this before it cools."

He laughed and they drank the tea. She also pulled out some food left from the day and they ate together undisturbed in the small shop.

The evening was growing colder and the young woman had not returned home. Her father began to watch the road intensely. He saw no one, not one traveler.

He looked at his wife and said, "She must be working on the shop. I am going into the village to see if she needs any help."

His wife agreed, and decided she would go with him, as the evening walk in the cold air would do her good. They both knew no harm had come to her. If there had been any trouble the others would have alerted them by now. But there was always that chance that defied odds, and he was not willing to take it.

Just then, the stranger's father and mother came to the door. They had brought some cakes the woman had baked and the man was eager to try out his new distilled drink on his old friend. Since the parents of the stranger had bought a neighboring farm, they had made a route to each other's place by building a nice path through a connecting field, shortening the distance down to about one quarter mile. It was a path lined with rock and timber and was easy to follow at night. In the day one could enjoy the flowers along the path.

The women named the path the "Thread of Joy" because it connected the two farms, households that enjoyed sharing their lives together.

The men decided they would walk into the village, as it would be faster. The women would stay and prepare the fresh cakes and make ready the drink. Both men laughed.

"This is warrior's duty," they boasted mockingly.

The women laughed at them and agreed. They would be much wiser to stay here where it was warm.

Then humorously, the men looked at each other and said, "Maybe we should stay where it is warm and try the drink; they could go into the village."

The women frowned and said they were only wasting time, if they did not hurry back, they may have to eat the cakes and drink the newly distilled drink themselves. At that note, the men were running and laughing like two young men for the road to the village. The women watched them go into the fading light just like two boys looking for mischief.

When the two men got to the road, they remained quiet, keeping a steady pace until they reached the village. Without speaking, it seemed they knew what the other was doing. They were both alert, aware of their surroundings. They quickly entered the village; most of the shops were closed or closing. They greeted a few shop owners leaving for their homes. As they approached the daughter's shop, it appeared to be closed. There was a horse with a heavy load standing in the front of the shop and a light coming from the inside. Slowly they approached, and their movements did not even frighten the horse. They did not recognize the horse. Looking through the window, which had a covering over it, they saw two figures not moving, just sitting.

The men looked at each other; they both knew what to do. Without speaking, the young woman's father headed to the side door. The stranger's father readied himself by the front door. Inside, the stranger and the daughter were talking quietly, then the stranger stopped speaking, he held a finger to his lips. The young woman's eye questioned his action and was just about to speak when she heard a whistle, which was the signal by one man to the other to enter the shop.

It all happened so fast. Upon hearing the whistle, the stranger began to stand, and both doors were quickly opened. By the time both of the men were standing in the light of the small shop, the stranger had moved with such speed as to put himself between the two intruders and the young woman. All she could do was stand against the wall where he had pushed her. In that same movement he had grabbed his staff and had it extended with his lead hand, he had also managed to draw a larger knife from somewhere on his body. The young woman was stunned. She had never seen such things.

Then she heard a voice, a surprised voice from the shadow of the front door.

"Son! My son! Is that you?"

The stranger never moved, never dropped his guard. Then the young woman's father moved into the light. He looked to his daughter.

"Are you alright?"

She could see he had the knife in his hand that the stranger had left for him. "It's okay, it's okay," she said. "It's him, the stranger, he came back, it's okay!"

At that moment, the stranger slowly moved back a step toward the young woman and slightly lowered his staff in the direction of her father at the side door. His knife hand still held steady toward the shadows of the front door. Slowly the figure emerged, small sword in hand; also slightly on guard. Then the young woman's father spoke to the other man.

He laughed and said, "I didn't know you still had that thing, you haven't lost your touch."

"Nor you," the other man said.

It was then the stranger lowered his knife hand and spun the blade back in the sheath behind his shoulder under his jacket.

"Father," the stranger said. "Is that you?"

His father moved toward him, he had already returned his sword to its scabbard just like the action of his son. For a moment, all was silent. Then he took a quick step and hugged his son. The son responded the same, but let out a groan when his father squeezed too hard. He let go, backed away and looked at his son, seeing him for the first time in two years. Then he saw the cuts that were healing, the bandaged hand, healed scars on the face and hands. A slow sigh of grief escaped from deep within him.

The father and daughter stood close together, as they witnessed the exchange between father and son. The son finally spoke.

"Father, what are you doing here?"

His father smiled and said, "Your mother and I live here. We own a farm next to my dear friend and his family."

"You, you live here? the son questioned. "How did this come to be?"

"It came to be, my son, because of you, because you carried out my request to give the information and gift to my friend. It happened because you kept your word. The rest is history we all can talk of in the future."

Then the daughter's father spoke up, "Come now, we have a real reason to celebrate; your homecoming young man, and that we are all finally together."

Then the daughter gasped and moved to the young man's side, "You are bleeding badly from your side, it is coming through your jacket. We must get you home and change those bandages. Can you make it?"

"Yes, it was nearly healed. I must have reopened it when I moved from the counter where we were sitting."

His father took a quick look at the wound, said nothing, but wrapped the present bandage tighter.

"That will do until we get to the house. Your mother is going to be very surprised, and I must say overwhelmed with joy to see you, maybe not in the present condition, but happy to see you," he said.

So they all straightened up the shop, picked up the stranger's pack; but he was no longer a stranger.

Now I have family and friends he thought to himself as they moved into the night. He tried to carry his pack, but his father took it.

"You carry this in the shape you are in?" he asked, surprised as he felt the weight.

"It is either that or make two trips."

The men led the horse and took turns carrying the pack while giving each other looks of amazement. The young man limped ahead of them at a good pace with the young woman at his side.

They talked between themselves. The old warriors followed, talking of the cakes and drink they soon would be enjoying. Then they all devised a plan for entering the house.

Just outside the farmhouse, they unloaded the burden from the horse and turned it into the pen by the barn. They carried all of the young man's belongings into the barn and threw out some feed for the horse.

The young man needed to rub the horse down before he left him, he said, "I must honor his service as he has been a good companion."

"But what of your wounds?" the young woman questioned him.

"Trust me," he said, "they will still be there when I have finished."

The two men looked at each other with a smile and nodded. The young man had truly come far in his understanding of life. After he tended to his horse, they all went to the house. The son remained on the porch for a moment while the two men and the daughter went in.

The women asked, "What took so long?"

Then the men asked if they drank all the distilled treasure. The women laughed and said there was plenty for everyone.

The daughter's father spoke first. "We got to the shop and some stranger was detaining our daughter. He would not let her go."

Then the son's father chimed in, "So, we burst in through both doors and rescued her."

The women were speechless.

They looked at the daughter, who had loosened her hair and messed it up a little before she came into the house. The young woman's mother jumped up and asked her daughter if she was okay. Then she turned and asked her husband, "What did you do to this stranger who held our daughter?"

"We have him tied up on the porch, we will give him to the authorities in the morning."

The women looked at each other.

The son's father said, "We had to rough him up a little, but he is alright."

Just then, the door burst open and the women screamed. Then there was silence. The men were trying not to laugh.

Unexpectedly, the mother recognized her son; her hand went to her mouth as she began to cry. She rose to her feet and ran to him, but stopped when he moved fully into the light.

Her eyes filled with anger and she turned and looked at the two men. "You did this?" She asked in an angry tone.

"No," the daughter's father spoke first. "I don't think we could, actually."

Then his own father went to the mother and hugged them both. Even the daughter's mother had tears in her eyes.

"So this is the one who made me this pendant. You are the traveler who waved at me, a year ago or more?" she asked in great surprise.

The young man looked quickly at her and said, "Yes, both answers are yes. I hope you can forgive me for bringing so much chaos into your lives."

She walked to him, gave him a hug, and said, "Welcome home young man, welcome."

He asked if he could sit, he felt tired and weak; he had not eaten all day until this evening, and then two rogue warriors looking for adventure rudely interrupted it. Everyone began laughing.

The daughter said, "We must attend to those wounds, we can do that as they prepare the food."

"What has happened to you?" his mother asked, looking at the cut on his face and the bandaged hand. Then she watched him limp to a chair. He took off his jacket and outer shirt slowly and carefully. Then he stopped, looking around shyly.

"It's okay," the daughter said, "It is okay."

"It's all right son, you have to get those treated," her father told him.

He relaxed and the daughter helped him raise the inner shirt over his head. The two women gasped, even the men muttered quietly. The young woman quickly prepared some warm water and soap, and gathered some herbs and fresh cloth wraps from the pantry.

The young man sat there with his head lowered, he finally spoke. "I am sorry to have troubled you all. I will go out to the barn and tend to this."

He started to rise but his father put a hand on his shoulder.

Before anyone could speak, the young woman blurted out, "You will do no such thing, you will sit right here and let me attend to you, do you hear me? You will not be going out to any barn. Now sit up straight so I can help you."

Everyone was surprised at her outburst, and both sets of parents just looked at their children and beamed with comical surprise.

The young woman's father spoke.

"You better do as she says son. I have seen her temper before and it is not a pretty sight to behold."

The room was filled with joyous laughter. The women went to work preparing some leftover food as the men were sitting down to enjoy their drinks and quietly talk; all stealing glances at the young man's body. His left side was almost black from bruising; there were cuts and old scars here and there. The worst was a wound on the side that had opened up again during the excitement at the shop. The young woman attended to them all with herb poultices and salves. They could not help but notice the tears that seemed to find their way down her cheeks as she swiftly worked on the young man's battered body. No one said a word. The young man's mother and father acknowledged the young woman's actions with a slight nod between them. This movement did not go unnoticed by the young woman's parents, as they smiled with delight.

When the young woman was finished and the young man had a clean shirt on, he moved to the table. The men said it was time for a drink.

He smiled and said, "I no longer drink, but please continue, have two for me."

His father frowned for a moment and acknowledged his son's words. The old warriors agreed they should drink for him so they each had another. The young woman said it was fine if they did. The young man told them all that he was better without drinking, at least for now; however, after some food he would like to share with them a short story.

"What a night," the young woman's father said, "action, adventure, food, drink, and stories. Life should be like this every day."

They all agreed, ate, and drank. The young woman made a special tea for the young man to help his wounds heal and give him back some strength.

When all had quieted down, the young man sat down on a cushion near the fireplace. The young woman wrapped a blanket on his shoulders, but he began to refuse it, and the young woman's mother said, "Please my young friend, let her help you. I have not seen her this quiet in a very long time."

He broke into his first genuine laugh of the day and the relief showed plainly on everyone's face.

"One question before your story," the young man's mother said. "We were in another village, a day's travel from here, and we heard a story of a young man who helped some farmers fight off some road bandits. Was that you?"

"Yes," he said. "If it were not for the farmers I might not be here today."

"That is not what they said," his father replied.
The young woman's father agreed.

"After the battle, they took me to the monastery because they knew I had spent many weeks with the monks teaching them some of the skills and crafts. The monks recognized me. They took me in and attended to my wounds; they would pray for me night and day. There was always someone attending me and praying over me. What happened to me there at the monastery is why I have returned."

The young woman stood up, looking at him with surprise and worry. "Have you become a monk, or are you going to?"

The young man smiled and held up his hand for her to stop. "Please," he said, "let me finish."

The young woman's mother touched her hand, and she sat back down. She was starting to show how exhausted she had become over the last few days. Then today, with all of the events that took place, she was starting to weaken, to fray apart like a used rope that was holding too much tension on it.

The young man continued.

"After I left here the first time, I traveled my usual route, trading at different farms, provinces, and villages. I began noticing more and more corruption in our society, not only from our political and religious leaders, but also from individuals who were cheating one another. Farmers were cheating each other, robbers were robbing farmers, the military and police were having their own power struggles. I have fought many battles helping people, and many people have helped me in battles during my travels. Then one day I came upon two monks, their cart had a broken wheel. I helped them fix the wheel on the cart and they offered me food and shelter for my efforts. I accepted.

"Upon arriving at the monastery, I was introduced to many of the other monks, as well as the head of the monastery. When the story was told of how I had helped the two stranded monks, I was readily accepted at their compound. After the evening meal, I walked with them in meditation. They would be in silent prayer to God as they moved at a slow pace through their beautiful gardens. Then they welcomed me in for the evening prayer before showing me to my room. They gave me a room with a small wooden bed, a table and chair, and a large candle for any reading to be done after dark.

"The next morning I awakened early and found them already doing chores before their morning meal. They told me to meet them at the hall at a given hour for the morning meal. I went into the field, out of their way, and began doing some stretching and a few sparring moves with feet and hands, as you had taught me, father."

His father nodded, but had a smile in his eyes.

"Then I began doing some stretching and exercises with my staff. As I turned in a circular motion, I saw several of the monks watching me. I stopped, bowed, and walked toward them. One of the monks went inside to bring out the head of the monastery, the abbot. I immediately began apologizing to them for interrupting their routine. I said I would quickly gather my things and leave them in peace. Then the abbot stopped me and said, 'Please do not leave; first, you have not offended us at all. We have often spoken of finding an exercise besides our labor here that would bring beneficial results, like balance and flexibility to enhance our regular activities. I feel your staff work may also help us against the bandits that often steal our goods as we go to and from the provinces. Would you consider staying for a while and teaching us some of these skills?'

"I was not only surprised but honored as well. I told him if he was interested I could stay for a couple of months or so; that way they would be proficient at these exercises and staff work. I told him I could also teach metal and woodwork for making tools, utensils, and knives for work around the monastery. 'Splendid,' the abbot said to me with a smile. I asked him if he had a forge. 'Yes, oh yes, and a wood shop,' he told me.

"I said excellent, and asked him if we should begin that day. 'Yes,' he said, 'we will have both morning and evening exercise and training periods. We will fit in the work with metal and wood during the normal workday. Now, let us attend to prayer and our morning meal.'

"This is how I came to be so acquainted with the monks. In the beginning, I felt it would be just another job. Then I would move on again. I was not mentally or emotionally prepared for the things to come. The more I involved myself in their way of life the more I began to have insights into the purpose of life. Prayer to them was not just thanking God before meals and at the end of the day. The more I prayed the more I began to open, like a flower blooming, or outer layers falling off.

"I am not sure how to describe it, but the more I participated in the prayers as a group and by myself the more I felt something taking place in me. Sometimes it was as if I were being released of many burdens, but then days later it was as if I had awakened some dark thing within me. Something filled with anger, an aggression toward everything I viewed as unjust; anything large or small at times could bring forth this anger. My workouts suffered because the emotion of anger disturbed my concentration. I began to accompany the monks on short journeys when they would purchase their supplies, or trade their goods. Ill-intentioned people often confronted them on these journeys. I watched them politely give up things, be pushed around, then my anger would grow and I would enter into the dispute. However, by then I was no talk, only brutal and swift force. I harmed many people and felt they deserved it. As you can see, I, too, was harmed by my own actions, and deserved it.

"As time went on, I began to notice the anger subsiding due to prayer, not aggressive action. I came to understand that true prayer was actually communication from the soul of a person to the creator of that soul; words that were not cluttered with selfish desires or worries, but words of hope, love, and the very yearning to speak to and know something of God. I was certain I should stay with the monks and live the lifestyle devoted to doing God's work as they did, for they chose a simple life, devoted entirely to seeking and worshiping God.

"They would rise with the sun and perform their prayers and day's work that was intended for their way of life. In the evenings, they would have debates and discussions on scriptures, the evening meal, and prayer. Then, until you slept, the time was yours to study, meditate, or do whatever you chose. I thought this would be the choice for me.

"One day when I was at the monastery recovering from the wounds, the abbot and I were walking in the garden. He would get me to take short walks with him; he said the light activity would help me to heal much faster as it would bring circulation to the injured areas. I asked him if I could join their group and he said it was possible, but he stopped and looked at me and said, 'I would like you to consider what I have to say before you make a choice to stay here. When you had been here for a few days after the farmers brought you to us, you were so badly injured we did not know if you would make it. There were days you would slip in and out of consciousness. Sometimes you would speak out, you said many things, but there was the name of a woman you spoke of more than once. I sent a few monks to close neighboring villages to look for her, but no one had heard of that name. I know there must be a very strong connection or you would not have mentioned her that often during your bouts with the fever that accompanied your many wounds. My friend, you must understand that there are many ways to serve God and do his bidding. Our life here at the monastery is just one way, it is not for everyone, and we are no better in the scheme of things than anyone who is devoted and seeks God in earnest. You have many talents my young friend.'

"I interrupted him, saying he had shown me so much, and it was there that I first felt peace in my entire being. 'That is good my friend,' the abbot replied, 'but in turn, you have shared with us your many skills of craftsmanship and self-protection. Though we do have somewhat of a different view of the severity of how these self-protection techniques are applied,' the abbot laughed. 'I feel in time you would be much happier outside of the monastic life. You have much to teach and share with others. You are always welcome here to visit and study if you feel the need. We would be very happy if you would come and share with us any new craftsmanship techniques. Most importantly, you must find this woman and attend to this matter within you, even if it takes your entire life. We would even be interested in meeting her should you choose to be a companion to her,' he finished, with a gleam in his eye.

"The abbot and I walked back toward the compound and he said to me, 'In a few more days you will be strong enough for your new journey. Please know that you are always welcome here, but you must start out before the winter season sets in. A farmer brought a horse as a gift of thanks from all of them and we will have it packed and ready for you to go. Stop in the village before you move on as the farmers want to see you. You have acquired many new friends in this area. With what you have shared with us, the roads here are now much safer than before.'"

The young man grew quiet for a minute then looked around the room. Everyone was touched by his story. The young woman just looked at him with compassion and uncertainty. He continued.

"After a few days had passed, I packed up and left the monastery. All the monks were out to see me before I left. I know I have a very close bond with them and the farmers too because they gave me a big welcome. The abbot had sent out a couple of monks a few days before to tell them when I would be passing through. We shared food and stories for a day and night. They gave me a place to rest for two days. Then I bid them well. They gave me food for the journey so I left them and came here. I had no idea that my parents were here. I came for you first. I had to know one way or the other if there was anything between us. Whatever the outcome, I was then going to return home and spend some time with my parents. Now it seems I do not have to keep making these journeys."

They all smiled. The men said they would drink one more to that. The air was filled with an irresistible vitality. There were no shadows of sadness to be seen.

The young woman then stood and walked toward the young man sitting there. She began to speak.

"Like you, I did not know how such a short meeting could affect a person so. The first night we met and you helped me clean up I felt a great connection to you. The moment you left, I realized I had not even gotten your name, and I felt much sorrow. As the days went by, I realized I had grown very fond of someone I may never see again. I grew angry in time and blamed you for my mistake of not asking your name and where you were from. I punished myself many times. I realized the emotion was not anger, but an emotion of attachment because I missed you, someone I did not even know. I felt I had fallen in love with you, but did not know. Now I know for sure it is true. When I realized it was your voice coming from above the counter tonight, I could not let you leave again without making my feelings known to you. Then when I saw the shape you were in, my heart just ached. Yes, yes, to answer your question. There is something great between us. I never want it to weaken but only to continue to grow in strength, as I hope we will. I feel I am in love with you and I never want you to leave like that again."

At that point, the two mothers looked at each other; their eyes wide with surprise at the daughter's boldness. Nevertheless, you could see their joy also, of what had been said.

The young man turned from the young woman and looked at his father. He nodded with a smile and then looked at the young woman's father and began to rise. The young woman's father said, "Do not get up, it is not necessary."

The young man turned and said, "I would very much like your blessing, for I do love your daughter, but I could not pursue such matters without your approval. Besides, it is as you told the two young men on the road that night that they had to address you before they could address your daughter." Everyone was smiling .

Then as it quieted the young man turned to the young woman, speaking slowly and clearly he said, "From the moment I saw you, your grace and discipline, and felt your energy, I was taken in by your beauty. You have not left my mind. You seemed to have taken up permanent residence in my heart, even in fever you do not leave me; the monks can attest to that."

There were sighs and more laughter before the young man resumed speaking to her.

"I had to leave as there were things I had to finish. I wanted to return with no distractions from the past. This way I will not have to leave you again. Now, I have returned in that manner. I choose to spend the rest of my days with you, living, sharing, and growing strong together. I feel there is much I can learn from you and a lot I can share with you. Would you be my companion through life?" he asked, lowering to her feet, kneeling in front of her.

This so honored the daughter she burst into tears, dropped to her knees, and said, "Yes, yes, I will."

At that point, both fathers cheered and both mothers laughed and cried at the same time.

The men shouted, "Time for a drink, there's more to celebrate."

The night continued to move along on the calm darkness of its journey toward the light of the coming day and a new beginning. The two families laughed and talked about the trials of life, and what beautiful opportunities the future seemed to hold.

His body began to stir. He began flexing and stretching. He was a little tired, but not drained. His eyes would not focus. Realizing it was still dark, he slowed his movements to let his eyes adjust to the darkness. Then, getting up, he kicked something with his foot, it sounded like a ceramic dish. He realized it was the teapot.

In that moment, he understood what had happened, and where he was. He quickly found a light switch, turning it on he remembered sitting down in his living room on his pillows to look at a teapot. He began to recall the vision, then saw the teapot: lid off, upright, undamaged on the floor next to the pillows.

The cobbler walked into the other room to look at the clock. The vision had lasted the entire day. It was well into the darkness of night; so instead of eating he just took off his clothes, remembering he had a couple of days off. He decided to go to bed hungry, get up early in the morning, and go into the desert for a hike. He wanted to try some deep meditation to see if any answers would reveal themselves to him about why people were seeking him out to understand their lives. Odd, he thought to himself, especially since I do not even understand my own life at times.

He climbed into bed. It felt good to relax without expectation. I do feel different, he thought to himself. Why, he did not know. Then his mind began to say a quiet prayer of thanks as he entered the realm of a peaceful sleep.

The next day he awakened early. It was still dark. He climbed out of bed, went to the window and checked the sky. The dark morning sky revealed stars mingling with small clouds. A slight breeze was moving the tree outside the window. He watched the tree's movements in the glow of the streetlights.

He put on a sweatshirt and pants and began to work out. After a good sweat, he ate a light breakfast, then packed some food and water into a bag.

Having shaved and showered, he got dressed and grabbed the bag of food and water, locked the house, and left for the desert. His drive to the desert would take about thirty minutes to get where he would watch the sun come up. Sunrises and sunsets were always special times for him. There was a small glow of orange on the horizon as he turned onto the dirt road into the desert. He drove a few miles until he could see the mound rising up out of the brush-covered desert.

He parked the truck and got out. He grabbed his bag, slung the strap over his shoulder, and began crossing a small ravine. Once he was on the other side, he hiked to the base of the hill. Adjusting the bag, he began the hike to the top of the hill. It was not very high, two or three hundred feet, but in the middle of a flat desert it looked like a giant wave moving across a calm ocean.

Once he arrived at the top, there was enough light to see his immediate surroundings. He found an open place in the brush on the east side of the hill. He took off his coat and laid it on the ground for a cushion and sat down facing east. He watched as the first rays of light began to chase the darkness from the land before him.

The small clouds that mixed with the sun's morning light provided colors of yellow, pink, and red. The morning was brilliant in its coming. The desert smell was always the most telling in the morning. Sage was the most prominent scent, but the gentle morning breeze carried hints of cedar and cactus flowers that were in bloom. He heard the cooing of turtle doves in the distance. A hawk was circling a stand of brush not far from the base of the hill. It already seemed to know where its daily meal would come from.

As he began to get comfortable watching the desert coming to life, he thought he heard a whisper, a quiet voice deep within his being. It was not the same loud, bold voice he usually heard that he often argued with about decisions pertaining to his life. That voice he associated with the ego. This voice was different, much calmer, a greater clarity of speech; not judgmental, just a calm quiet matter-of-fact feeling resonating with its words. He stopped moving, became still, and began to focus on the voice.

All the questions you have, all this confusion and disappointment you feel, is not what you presently think it is. Now, after putting away the books that have been your guideposts for years, you have come to learn the difference between knowledge and wisdom. Knowledge is just information whereas wisdom is information organized through the experiences you have had.

The people who come to you seeking answers, are not people you perceive them to be at all. They are physical manifestations of questions you, yourself, have. You are not guiding others—not in the way you think. You will benefit the whole of humanity by finally understanding yourself.

Moreover, by understanding yourself, you are helping others by just being who you truly are: the gentle soul full of compassion who has learned the difference between knowledge and wisdom.

You are not the great and knowing philosopher with answers for others as you once questioned. All of these people, these topics, and these visions of actions and activities, are nothing more than scenarios for you to come to an understanding and peace within yourself.

These are the questions that have been hidden away deep inside you, because of the experiences you have had. You must realize by now that it was somewhat astonishing that people you did not even know were looking to you for wisdom and guidance; something your ego loved and instantly attached a great importance to.

This is why there was much disharmony within you. The ego would not let go of another chance to become stronger within.

Now that you know the truth and are beginning to feel a peace slowly growing inside of you, things will begin to become different than before. Your feelings, thoughts, and actions will be coming from your source, not from your ego. The ego will step in at times and try to regain its hold, but it will not establish itself as it previously has as long as you continue to recognize your true nature and the nature of other things. It will not be easy, but the answers to any questions you have will be revealed. Learn to listen with all of your being, not just your ego. The truth is revealed when you hear, see, and feel all things with every cell of your being.

By the way, you will also come to realize that the people who come to you for work are not actually interruptions of your daily tasks. Every one of them is a gift, bringing gifts.

They are providing you with an opportunity to work in a trade you love, to express your passion of artful creativity while doing something you feel is work. It is providing a service for the good of the whole. If you take a moment and think about this, you will see that without them, you would be doing something that does not find harmony within you at all. This is only the beginning.

As the voice quieted, he could feel the warmth of the morning sun upon his face. Slowly he began to study the beauty of the scene that lay before him. It was obvious now;

it was the same way with the business world he toiled in. All the pieces are moving and interacting with one another; however, we are just too closely involved to see the function of the whole.

He finally realized this new information. There were many personal changes he would have to make, and this would not be easy. But, then again, maybe it was not supposed to be easy. Man, including himself, had become intellectually and analytically aloof, but spiritually poor.

The believer needed to be regained.

A band of wild horses roaming the area came running up out of the small ravine at the base of the hill where he was sitting. This new activity changed the focus of his intention onto the horses. While watching the horses move about, checking the grass for a morning meal, he began eating the food he had brought with him. An early morning picnic, he thought to himself.

The young horses ran, bucked, and played as the others spread out and began to graze. The herd stallion moved to higher ground to keep a more vigilant eye on his family.

The cobbler finished his picnic, the words of the voice echoing in his mind, especially the last phrase.

This is only the beginning.

If all of this information was true, he thought, he had a lot of work cut out for himself. He knew he had the discipline but he would have to make himself focus on this new gift of knowledge. If he could focus, he could possibly become happier.

No, no, that's not the way, he thought. He could become at peace with himself, then happiness would naturally follow. Things were truly beginning to happen. This is what must be done.

He quickly stood, gathered his things, took one more look around at the beautiful scene before him, said a short prayer of thanks to God, and walked back to his truck.

As he was driving back from the desert something kept compelling him to just go back to work, but he fought the idea because he wanted the rest of the day to himself. Then he realized this may have something to do with the statement,

"This is only the beginning."

On the drive back to town he thought about the information the voice had given him. He saw how man had created his own chaos, for we all are nothing but children. Children are given books and toys, told stories, and this gives them their foundation to grow into adults. This brought a laugh from him for he saw the folly in the words alone. We are all still children; still receiving stories, toys, and books. One thing we were leaving out was the wisdom of the voice within each of us. We were being distracted from God and the love, and this is where intention should be.

We do not have to stop the activities we enjoy; just change the intentions. The intention should be on God and His love first. The work, play, all things of enjoyment will be cherished because you are sharing with the creator, not detaching yourself from the source of all things. You become one with the whole.

He came to the main road and turned toward town, and work, without hesitation. He could feel himself surrendering to this inner voice trying to guide him. The town, like the desert, had its morning rituals well underway. People were running across the streets with coffee and morning sweets.

Some people were buying newspapers at the stand and discussing the events of the opened pages before they had to answer to work's beckoning call.

He parked his truck and stepped onto the sidewalk where he brushed the dust and dirt from his clothing before entering the shop.

The shop was already opened for business. Everyone was surprised to see him since he still had two days off. He smiled and said he felt like he needed to be back.

He put on his apron, gathered his tools, and began sorting the boots and shoes for his days work.

Gifts, he heard the voice say, gifts. Smiling to himself he thought, it's already working.

"Excuse me," he heard a female voice and looked toward the counter. He set down the pair of shoes and walked to the counter to address the customer. Laying on the counter was a small canvas roll tied with a leather thong.

"Your co-worker said you may be interested in some hand tools."

He glanced quickly at the woman, but his eyes immediately switched back to the tools.

"I'm always interested in hand tools," he replied with a smile.

He untied the leather thong and unrolled the canvas case. He saw that they were indeed tools used for shoe repair. Without looking up he asked, "Where did you acquire these?"

As he began to handle the tools, the woman responded, "I thought you may like them back."

Shocked at her reply, he looked up at the woman's face just as an amber lock of hair broke loose and swept across her gray-green eyes.

The tool he was holding fell from his hands onto the counter. All he could do was stare.

She reached out, took his empty hand in hers, and smiled. "We have been looking for you everywhere."

Then a younger version of the woman walked up to the counter and smiled. Behind her amber hair were his eyes shining back at him. He looked down at the woman's hand holding his. He looked back into the eyes of the girl.

"How could this be?" he asked out loud.

Then from deep inside, and this time very clear, he heard the voice answer his question.

The gift of life has many lessons and these lessons are the gifts. This is only the beginning.